Swingin' on the Old Time Gate

"What's the matter?" I asked, regretting it even as I said it. "Scared?"

Matty stood up, but he didn't get mad, like I thought he would. "Yeah, I'm scared Richie," he said, "and I think if you had any sense, you'd be scared too. Face it, babe. You think it'll be all great sounds and a good time. But I tell you this. If we get into trouble, nobody's gonna bail us out but us. I worry about that, but it isn't what bothers me most."

"What does, then?" I asked.

"It's this one-way Gate in Time business. Don't you see that if we don't like it back then, it's just tough. We *can't* get back!"

"We can always find the Future Gate," I said, sounding surer than I really was. "And I'll tell you this. I'm going alone or with you. But believe it, I'm going."

"A dandy story with a nimble twist."
—*Publishers Weekly*

"Humor and deftly handled dialogue."
—*School Library Journal*

Tune In Yesterday

T. Ernesto Bethancourt

RL 5, IL 5+

TUNE IN YESTERDAY

*A Bantam Book / published by arrangement with
Holiday House*

PRINTING HISTORY
Holiday House edition published March 1978
2 printings through August 1979
Bantam edition / April 1981

ISBN 0-553-13324-1

Published simultaneously in the United States and Canada

---

*Bantam Books are published by Bantam Books, Inc. Its trade-
mark, consisting of the words "Bantam Books" and the por-
trayal of a bantam, is Registered in U.S. Patent and Trademark
Office and in other countries. Marca Registrada. Bantam
Books, Inc., 666 Fifth Avenue, New York, New York 10103.*

PRINTED IN THE UNITED STATES OF AMERICA

0 9 8 7 6 5 4 3 2 1

*For the jazzmen who still remain, and those
yet to come, may you always have
as attentive and sensitive an audience
as the author has found in Margery Cuyler.*

Acknowledgment

Research as to what bands were playing, their sidemen and styles of playing, as well as physical descriptions and locations of nightclubs on the "street" the week of February 8, 1942, was provided by Alan Cary of New York City, friend, scholar, jazz historian, and plectrum banjoist *extraordinaire*. The Horn of Plenty club is fictional.

Contents

1

Hey, Look Me Over

Branford, Long Island, is an old town. It was founded
before the American Revolution. Nowadays, there's no
trace of the family that founded it. There hasn't been a
Branford living in Branford since before World War II.
Come to think of it, there isn't too much happening in
Branford, period. Garden City, which is nearby, has a
bunch of New York City department store branches and
a college. All we've got in Branford is two lonely historical plaques. Maybe that's why the Bicentennial celebration we had struck me as a bad joke. But being a member
of the Branford High School band, I had to play and wear
this stupid outfit they ran off for the pageant.

I don't mind our regular band outfits too much. They're
silly looking, but I never saw a band outfit that wasn't.
These Bicentennial outfits were something else, though.
They dressed us all up like Revolutionary War soldiers.
It wasn't a bad idea, but the costumes were so cheapo-
sleazo, I felt like a turkey marching in mine.

1

First off, the Jaycees, who thought up the whole thing, wouldn't buy us real boots. We had to wear our regular shoes with these phony lace-up tops over them. But the lace-ups were shiny imitation black leather, and all our band marching shoes were brown.

So there I was in a sleazy costume, wearing black tops and brown bottoms to my shoes. And I wasn't the only one. I thought I looked dumb until I saw Billy Koenig marching beside me with his tops over white sneakers. Man, talk about tacky!

We were playing for Branford's big-deal history pageant, which is another bad joke. Way back in the early days of the Revolution, some second-rate Colonial soldiers and an out-at-the-elbows colonel retreated from the British across what's now downtown Branford. Can you imagine having a parade to commemorate a bunch of losers? But that's Branford for you.

We even had a reviewing stand. Art Maloney, the mayor, was there, along with the Jaycees. They must have raided the ROTC classes at one of the colleges nearby. There were a bunch of guys about my age on the stand, wearing those cupcake uniforms ROTC has. The only thing tackier than the toy soldiers was all the fathers in their old uniforms from World War II, Korea, and Vietnam. Hardly any of the fathers still fit into their old uniforms or still had complete ones to wear. So you'd see some guy in an army jacket and hat, but he'd be wearing regular slacks and Hush Puppies on his feet. They looked like a troop of poverty-level Boy Scouts.

What saved the parade from being a complete bust was Al Foster's dog, Jumbo. Jumbo is a huge mutt. Looks like he's made from the spare parts of six other very ugly dogs. He hangs out in front of Al's Bar & Grill in good weather, and inside when it's cold or raining. Al has a collar and license for him; it's not like Jumbo was a stray. Al Foster jokes around that Jumbo's father was a horse, not a dog. You look at this mutt and you can believe it.

Anyway, we had marched up to the reviewing stand and stopped. It was all part of the unveiling of "The Spirit of Branford," which is a statue in bronze of a Revolutionary soldier with his rifle at his side. The unveiling was dumb, too. Everybody in Branford had seen the statue two days before. Workmen had brought it in from New York City and bolted it to the concrete base. After the whole town had seen the workmen bolt it down, they threw this tarpaulin over it. So when Art Maloney pulled the cord on the canvas cover at the end of his speech, everyone was supposed to go "Ooooh!" like they never saw it before.

Art finished his speech about our brave ancestors. Then with a big flourish he pulled the cord as he said, "Ladies and gentlemen. I give you 'The Spirit of Branford'!" It got a lot of oohs and ahs, all right. Because when the canvas slid away, there was good old Jumbo underneath it. Taking a dump. Meantime, all the kids in the band were trying not to break up laughing.

I looked back to the drum section and my main buddy, Matty Owen. He was trying not to laugh and still stand up straight with his bass drum strapped on. It must have got to Mr. Green, our band director, and shook him up pretty good. He whistled the band to attention and called for number seventeen. Number seventeen on our band charts is *Hey, Look Me Over*. So, off we marched down Branford street blaring out *Hey, Look Me Over*, while most of Branford was doing just that with Jumbo's call to nature. Art Maloney still stood there with the tarpaulin cord in his hand and a dumb look on his face. The ROTC guys on the stand were shifting from foot to foot and wondering what to do or say.

None of this bothered Jumbo, who just finished his business and then walked off toward Al's Bar & Grill. As we passed out of sight of the reviewing stand, I heard some wiseass try to get up a round of applause for Jumbo, but it didn't catch on.

By the time we'd finished the march, at the old Revolutionary War cemetery at the edge of town, I was glad it was all over. I sat down on the nearest tombstone and took the tuba off my neck. It was there I lost my wallet. I remember it clearly. I'd taken out my wallet to pay Matty Owen the coupla bucks I owed him.

Matty is my main man. We both play in the three bands that Branford High has: marching, orchestra, and dance band. In the orchestra, I play string bass; Matty plays timpani and triangle. In the dance band, he plays the drums and I play electric bass.

Matty had loaned me a few bucks the night before the parade. We wanted to see a Charles Bronson flick at the drive-in. He'd gotten his '63 Chevy going again. I think he takes it apart and puts it together once a week, just for fun. I was tapped, so he laid a few bucks on me. Matty's that way; he don't care diddly about money. I guess it's because his old man has lots of coins. Matty's dad sells electronic equipment. I suppose that the Owens are the richest black family in Branford—probably better off than most of the white families as well.

Matty's a hustler and a promoter. He's always got some scheme going. Sometimes his schemes pay off, too. Not that he cares. I think he promotes mostly for the fun of doing it. Like today, at the cemetery, he had stashed a six-pack of beer on ice where he knew we were going to end up at the parade's end.

We unzipped a couple of beers. And it must have been when I paid Matty back that I put my wallet on top of a tombstone, instead of back in my pocket. I wouldn't even have known where to look for it later, but Matty drew my attention to the tombstone I was sitting on.

"Richie, how can you stand the smell where you're sitting?" he asked.

"What are you talking about?" I said.

"Can't you see the name on the tombstone?" Matty laughed.

I looked behind me and read what was written on it. It was blurry, but still pretty legible:

> HERE LIE THE REMAINS OF
> ABNER PEW, FREEMAN.
> DIED JUNE 16, 1778.
> HIS VALOUR IN SAVING THE LIFE
> OF NATHANIEL BRANFORD
> WON FOR HIM HIS FREEDOM.
> MAY THE FREEDOM BORN OF BATTLE
> ENDURE LONGER THAN THIS STONE. R.I.P.

"Get it?" Matty said. "Pew . . . phew!"

It was a lame joke, and I soon forgot it. But when I got home, a little after dark, I knew the cemetery was the only place I could have left my wallet. Then I was glad I knew where to go. My mom wasn't home; she'd left a note on the kitchen table and a frozen dish in the microwave oven. I didn't bother to take off my turkey band outfit. I just took a flashlight from the kitchen and pedaled my bike over to the cemetery again, which is how I found myself poking around a graveyard, looking for Abner Pew's tombstone. I found it, no sweat, and also my wallet. But I don't mind saying that I was glad to be out of the graveyard. Not that I believe in ghosts and all that crap. Still and all, a cemetery at night isn't what I'd call a swift place to be.

I knew there was something wrong the minute I got outside the graveyard and onto Route 25-A. Inside the town limits, 25-A is called Branford Street. Once you're outside the town, it turns back into 25-A. I thought at first I'd taken a wrong turn of some sort. The road I'd come out on was a dirt road. I went back inside the cemetery and made sure I'd come out the main gate, not the back, which leads to some woods.

No mistake. Not only was there no blacktop or concrete road, my bike was gone. An almost brand-new ten-speed Peugeot I got for Christmas a year ago. Swearing to myself, I started down the strange dirt road heading for town on foot, for the second time that day.

I guess the only thing that kept me from freaking out completely was the dreamlike quality everything had that night. The moonlight, the stillness, all combined to make it seem unreal. And the same way a dream can scare you, but you still feel safe, was the reason I didn't panic. And the feeling wasn't so much of everything being strange and different. It was subtler than that. It was the feeling of everything being the same, yet somehow different. Things were missing.

The traffic signal at Cedar St. and 25-A wasn't there. I don't mean it was blown out; it just wasn't there. All the highway lights were out, too. And I couldn't see the passing headlights from cars on the Long Island Expressway, either. And that's the reason that the light is there on Cedar. It's an entrance to the L.I.E.

As I got further into where the town should have been, it got even spookier. I couldn't find the houses of people I knew who lived right on Branford St. I also knew that for the amount of time I'd been walking, I should have come to the turnoff for my own house. I know that it sounds goofy, but the whole town seemed to have disappeared!

I kept walking, and in a few minutes found myself in the middle of this dirt road, facing the old church that had burned down when I was just a kid. But it wasn't burned out. It looked brand new. There were some houses clustered around the church, but none that I recognized, except for the old courthouse. At least that was where it should have been, facing the church.

Nearby, there was a long, wide, two-story building with a light shining from the lower floor. When I got close, I smelled a strong scent of horses. I checked, and sure enough there was a stable behind the big structure. As I came up to the window where the light was coming from, I heard a steady, rhythmic squeak-squeak. I looked up and cut on my flashbeam. It was a hand-painted, swinging sign that read BRANFORD INNE & TAVERNE, WINES AND SPIRITS, FOOD AND LODGING, B. MILLS. PROP. I kept my flashlight beam on the sign for a minute. No doubt it said BRANFORD INNE. So this *had* to be Branford. But not any Branford I'd ever seen. And the lettering was strange, too. Like the script on Abner Pew's tombstone. I came up close to the window where the light was coming from and peeked in.

The bottom floor was all one big room. There was a fireplace with the remains of a fire still going. The hearth and fireplace together looked big enough to barbecue a Volkswagen in. There were gangs of shiny copper utensils all around it on the wall. And sitting at a long table, leaning over what looked like a ledger book of figures, sat this middle-aged, red-faced guy. He was wearing an outfit that would have been right in place in the Bicentennial parade, earlier. But his getup looked real. No sleazo stuff. He was wearing a leather apron over it, and he had an old-fashioned quill pen in his hand. An inkwell stood nearby on the table.

He was really wrapped up in his figuring. When I went and peeked through the window, a dog somewhere nearby began to bark. He didn't look up. I watched him for a few seconds longer, then retraced my steps back to the cemetery and Abner Pew's gravestone. But this time, when I walked out the gate, my bike was there again. And when I pedaled back into town, everything was normal and where it should have been.

I was really shaken and made it over to the Burger

King to see if Matty was hanging out. When he gets the Chevy going, that's where he goes on week-nights. He wasn't there, and I didn't feel like talking to the kids who were. I went on home.

My mother was still up when I got in. She was watching the 11:00 news on TV. She looked up when I let myself in, then went back to her TV. I saw she had a tall glass of what looked like Pepsi or Coke on her TV table. I knew better. It was her usual: half Diet Pepsi and half whiskey. From the looks of her, it wasn't the first by a long shot. The ashtray in front of her was filled to overflowing, and there were already a few ring marks from glasses on the tabletop. She was wearing a housecoat and slippers and had taken off her wig. She must have come home a few minutes after I'd left for the cemetery.

I don't know what to do about Mom's boozing. It started out small, just after she and Harry, my dad, broke up, about five years ago. But each year, it seems to get worse. And there's no talking to her about it. I've tried. She gets all up in the air and tells me I'm just a kid, and who am I to lecture my mother? I tried to talk to Harry about it; I see him almost every weekend. But it's harder to talk to Harry than Mom.

In fact, I find it hard to call my dad Harry. But when he and Mom got the divorce, Harry changed his whole way of life. At first, when I'd go visit him in New York City on weekends, we'd go to ball games and shows. Stuff like that. It was a groove. Harry never did that when he and Mom were still together. But after a few months, we went places with Harry's new girlfriend, Helene.

I guess that hearing me call him Dad in front of Helene made him feel too old. I'm over six feet tall now, and even then I was taller than Harry. To make it worse, Helene isn't too much older than me. When we went places together, people thought that Helene and I were together and that Harry was our father. That's when Harry had me stop calling him Dad.

And we really don't talk. Oh sure, we say our "How's it going's?" and he asks me about school. Then we're off to someplace with Helene, and there's no chance to talk. And each weekend that I stay over in the city, I come back to find Mom bombed out of her head, with the house looking like a junkyard. Once when I came back early, I found some dude about fifty years old crashed in my bed. It didn't make coming home a good feeling. It hasn't felt good for years now. But what the heck, it could be worse. I mean like Matty. His mom died two years ago, and his oldest sister is running the house. And let me tell you, Loretta Owen is a monster pain in the tail.

I was glad Mom didn't feel like talking. I hit the shower, cleaned up, and went to bed. I didn't watch TV, either. It had been a long, weird day, and I was tired. I crashed real hard. No dreams, no nothing. It wasn't until I passed the "Spirit of Branford" downtown, on my way to Saturday band practice, that I remembered my weird walk the night before.

I made a note to myself to talk to Matty about it, on the quiet. I didn't know, you see, if it had all really happened, or if I was losing my grip and I'd been hallucinating. I wasn't even sure I wanted to talk to Matty about it. After all, it *was* kind of strange. But I did, and I have to say it was either the dumbest or the smartest move I've ever made.

2

I'm Just Mild About Harry

"Gilroy . . . Gilroy!" I was so preoccupied with thinking about last night that I hadn't heard Mr. Davis calling the roll.

"Here, Mr. Davis!" I hollered.

"Yes, I can see that your body is here, Richie," said Mr. Davis. "I was merely wondering when you were going to honor us with the rest of you. We do like to have a *full* band at rehearsals . . ."

He went on like that for a few minutes. Mr. Davis is a sarcastic dude. I don't know why he ever got into teaching kids if he hates them so much. Or maybe he didn't start out mean, and he got that way over the years. I think if I had to spend all that time with some of the kids I know, it'd turn me mean, too. He finished up his monologue on what a goof I am, and we settled down for the afternoon's practice session. It went smooth enough until we had a few rough spots on the *Washington Post March*. Mr. Davis was chewing out the whole band.

"Once more, you crowd of fumblers," he said, "take it from letter A and up to the next sixteen measures. And this time, I want to hear the clarinets, not a noise some animal would make."

I guess the animal crack made somebody think about yesterday and Jumbo's contribution to Branford's Bicentennial celebration. Because when the clarinet section was due to come in, some clown started in barking like a dog. You could see by how red in the face he got that Mr. Davis hadn't forgotten, either. He got so pissed off that he canceled the rest of the session. I caught up with Matty down in the locker room, where he was putting away the bass drum.

"Hey, babe," I said, "who was that barking? It sure got to Davis."

"It was behind me," Matty said. "It was probably Koenig again. Davis is gonna kick him out of the band completely if he doesn't take care."

"No big loss," I said. "Koenig couldn't blow his nose. He's a clown, too. Did you see him yesterday with the sneakers on?"

"Richie, once I strap on that damn bass drum, I can't even see my own feet, let alone anyone else's. He was wearing sneakers, huh?"

"Yeah. White ones. I thought I was bad with brown shoes, but Koenig . . ."

Matty shook his head, grinning. "Listen, man. It takes all kinds. Even the weird kinds," he said.

Which reminded me about the night before. We walked out of the school and into the parking lot. Matty had the Chevy running again, and we took off for the Burger King. Along the way, I asked him, "Matty, what's the weirdest thing that ever happened to you?"

"You mean, outside of hanging out with you?"

"Very swift," I said. "I mean, have you ever had something so strange happen that you were afraid to tell any-

one? I mean, afraid people would think you'd gone flaky
if you told them about it?"

Matty glanced over at me from the driver's side. I
guess he could tell by the look on my face that I wasn't
jiving.

"Why don't you just tell me, and I'll tell you if I think
you're nuts?" he said. So I did.

When I finished my story, we were already at the
Burger King. We didn't go in. We sat in the car while
Matty asked me more about my strange walk. After I
convinced him that I was straight in the head, he sat
back and thought for a while.

"Richie," he said, "there's two possible answers, as I
see it. Either you've lost your marbles, or it all really
happened. From talking to you, you don't seem any crazi-
er than usual. I think it really happened."

I can't tell you what a relief it was. I had thought for a
few minutes Matty was going to be polite and then make
some kind of excuse to split. Like when somebody does
something way out and embarrassing. I don't mind saying
that for some time last night, I wasn't too sure I *hadn't*
slipped a gear someplace in my head. So he took me by
surprise when he said, "What you going to do about it,
Richie?"

"What is there to do?" I asked. "If it happened, it
happened. Today, it all seems so far away, that town that
was Branford, yet wasn't, and the guy in the Branford
Inne . . . I don't know."

"Hey, I got an idea!" said Matty, snapping his fingers.
"Let's go over to the Historical Society. They open on
Saturdays?"

"Sure. Mrs. Krendler has been keeping the place open
six days since the Bicentennial started. What do we want
to go there for?"

"Just a funny idea," said Matty, cranking up the Chevy.
"If I'm wrong, you call tell me *I'm* nuts. Deal?"

"Deal!"

You know, sometimes people look like what they do for a living. You look at some guy, you say, "That's a carpenter," and he is. Same thing with Mrs. Krendler. She was a history teacher at Branford High for years and years. Then when she retired from teaching, she set up the Branford Historical Society. It's really just a double storefront on Jarvis Street, but she's done a lot with the inside. It's all antique furniture from the Revolutionary War and around then. The kids in town joke that Mrs. Krendler is so old that it's really her living room furniture she's got in the little museum she keeps.

But she's a nice old lady. To me, anyway. My mom says when she had Mrs. Krendler for history in high school, that she was some kind of tough on tests and grades. And Mom says she was old, even then. So I guess you'd tend to believe Mrs. Krendler when she teaches history. She looks like she was there. She gave me a big hello when Matty and I came into the museum.

"Well, well. If it isn't Claudia Green's boy! How are you, Richard?"

"Just fine, Mrs. Krendler. This is my friend, Matty Owen. He wants to ask you some questions about . . . What did you want to know, Matty?"

"How do you do, Mrs. Krendler," says Matty in his best con man's voice. "I'm delighted to meet you. I was just curious about how old the town of Branford really is, and what it used to be like way back then."

Mrs. Krendler lit up like a Christmas tree. I guess she doesn't get many people coming into the museum. And I know for a fact that no kids from my age group go in there at all. She went to a big, old map on the far wall, above a spinning wheel. She put her finger on a point, and we both went over to look. She went into a spiel like the guys that sell records on the TV commercials.

"Now, this is Long Island the way it looked over two

hundred years ago. Here is Branford. As you can see, it wasn't ever a large town. It was founded in 1756 by Bertram Mills. It wasn't called Branford then, though. Originally, the town was only a stopping place for the horse-drawn coaches that carried passengers and mail into New York City. The town was called Mills Hostel until the Revolution. That was when Nathaniel Branford settled here and fought the battle we commemorated only yesterday, downtown. By the way, did you like the new statue?"

I almost didn't hear her. My head was spinning. If Branford was once Mills Hostel, then the sign I'd seen on my strange walk made a lot of sense. Maybe the guy I'd seen through the window was Bertram Mills, himself! But how? And why?

"Yeah, sure, Mrs. Krendler," I said. "Swell statue."

"Pardon me, Mrs. Krendler," put in Matty, "but do you have a larger map of Branford itself, about the time of the Revolution?"

"Of course, young man," she said stiffly. "I have one of the best collections of town plans on Long Island. The history departments of both C. W. Post and Hofstra Colleges consult me regularly."

She went over to a lectern-thing that could have come out of an old church or a courthouse, and began going through the pages of a very big, very old book. It was bound in leather and had brass hinges on the spine. It was so old, the leather was flaked and almost like cardboard.

"Here we are," she chirped. "This is exactly how Branford looked in 1790."

I came closer and looked over her shoulder. I nearly dropped my teeth. The old-timey lettering was a bit hard to read, but there was no mistaking the little cluster of buildings indicated on the map page. It was an exact duplicate of the "Branford" I'd walked through the night before!

Matty and I made some more conversation with Mrs. Krendler, but I couldn't tell you what it was about. From the time I saw that map, all I could think about was how? And why?

After telling Mrs. Krendler I'd say hello to my mom for her, we went back to Matty's car. We didn't take off. We sat there in silence for a time, then Matty said, "I guess you're not nutty after all, Richie. From what those maps show, and what the old doll says, you were actually in Branford two hundred years ago."

"It's a relief, I guess," I said. "But there's so much I don't understand. How did I get there? Why did it happen at all?"

Matty started up the car and eased it into gear. We moved off Jarvis St. and onto Branford, headed out of town.

"If it happened once, it could happen again," Matty said. "Let's go take a look at the cemetery. Maybe if we retrace your moves, we can find out just what did happen."

"Hold on," I said. "I can't go out there now. It's after one o'clock, and I have to meet Harry down near the Square."

"Rats!" said Matty. "I forgot. Is this one of the weekends you're going to stay over in the city?"

"No," I said. "We were only going out to catch the automobile show at the Nassau Coliseum. I should be back in town by dinner time."

Matty swung the Chevy around, made a slightly illegal U-turn, and headed back downtown. I jumped out at Main and Branford. As we pulled up, I could see Harry's Mercedes-Benz convert parked in front of Al's Bar & Grill. Harry was sitting there waiting. I crossed the intersection and came up on the passenger side and opened the door. It startled Harry. I guess he was expecting me to come from the other direction, from band practice, like I usually do when I meet him.

"Hi, kid," he chirped, once he recovered. "Howsitgoing?"

"Great, Harry," I answered, like he really cared. "Howsitgoing with you?" Like I really cared, anymore.

"Swell, Richie. Say, look. Are you truly set on going to the Coliseum today?"

"Well, I wanted to see their collection of classic cars . . ."

Harry squirmed a bit. I have to give him credit for that much. I knew he was going to try to weasel out of going. Hell, I didn't mind. But there's this game you got to play. I have to look disappointed, and he's got to act as though the only thing in the world he wanted was to spend the day with me. But I really did want to see the classic cars. And this was the first time in I don't know how long I had a chance to see Harry without Helene being there. I could have let Harry off easy, but for some reason I wanted to sweat him a little before I said all right, forget it. Harry was glancing at his watch. Must be on a tight schedule, I thought.

"Look, Richie," he said hurriedly. "I'd love to make it. I mean, I have been looking forward to it, myself. But to tell you the truth, this business thing has come up. I have to get back to town. So here . . ."

Harry rummaged through the papers in the glove compartment and came up with two tickets to the auto show. I all of a sudden felt guilty about making Harry squirm. He really had bought the tickets. He must have actually had some business thing come up. He opened his wallet and took out two twenties.

"Listen, Richie," he said, "why don't you take a friend and have dinner on me afterward? I really feel bad about this, but you know, if I don't take care of business, those checks to your mom will stop coming in . . ."

"All right, I get the message, Harry," I said. "No big thing. My pal Matty has his car going again. We can make it out there OK."

He looked visibly relieved. He didn't have to say that about the checks he sends to me and Mom. I know when they come in and how much they're for. For the past few months, I'd been depositing the checks at the bank and making out the bills. Mom gets terribly depressed each month about check time. I suppose it reminds her that she and Harry are all over for good. So she gets stoned. After she blew two checks in a row that way, I started heading her off at the pass, so to speak.

But like I said, I saw that this time Harry wasn't kidding. He'd bought the tickets, so I figured he really had planned on going with me. For me, that was enough. The idea that he was planning on a day with me and no Helene somehow made me feel a lot warmer toward him. I guess that's why when I got out of the car I said, "Thanks for the tickets, Dad."

Harry gave me a look that had no name on it. "Sure thing, son," he said. Then he took off.

I went across the street to the drugstore to telephone Matty, once I saw Harry's Mercedes turn the corner. I got Matty at home, and he said he could make it to the show. He'd pick me up in ten minutes in front of the drugstore. I looked through some magazines by the rack while I was waiting. No, not *Playboy*, *Penthouse*, or *Hustler*. They keep those behind the counter in Branford. I was looking through *Motor Trend*, *Car and Driver*, and *Sports Cars Illustrated*. I was about to get into an article on a restored Duesenberg SJ when I saw the Mercedes come around the corner and pull up near Al's.

It was Harry, all right. I put down the magazine and was ready to run across the street to him. Maybe the business thing had fallen through, and he could make it after all! I watched him go into Al's. I figured he was going to make a phone call to the house. Harry won't come to the house anymore. He never knows when Mom is going to make a scene, or what shape she'll be in once he gets there.

I was halfway out of the front door of the drugstore when he came out again. He wasn't alone. She was blond, in her early twenties, and a dynamite looker. She was also most definitely not Helene. From the way they were looking at each other, and by the way Harry helped her into the car, I was pretty sure they weren't off to take care of any business deal, either.

They drove off. I stood there feeling like a complete fool. I was glad I hadn't dashed out to greet Harry. I would have screwed up his whole afternoon plot. What a gag! Harry wasn't content with having Helene on the line. He was branching out. And using me as an excuse to Helene to get away and do it! I've seen some cheap shots, but this one really hurt. It wouldn't have hurt so much if I hadn't been feeling so kindly toward Harry just then. I'd even called him Dad!

Matty pulled up in front of the drugstore. I hopped in, and we rode in silence out to the Coliseum. Matty tried to make some chatter, but once he saw I wasn't in a talking mood, he turned on the eight-track, and we listened to the Glenn Miller Band on the way out.

I'll tell you, there's something about Swing and Jazz from the '40's. I can't hear it and stay mad or upset. There's such a joy to the music. Not that the Miller Band was the greatest. I mean, it was a good, commercial sound in its day, but there were a lot of other bands saying more. Trouble is, some of the real great bands, like Jimmy Lunceford, didn't do that much recording. And very few of the really great ones are on reissued albums, the way Miller, Artie Shaw and Benny Goodman are. You have to buy the original records from collectors. Too expensive. Matty has some, and after we transferred them to tape, he had to put them away someplace safe from his two younger sisters.

Just as we pulled into the Coliseum parking lot, the tape swung into the Miller Band doing Jerry Gray's arrangement of *String of Pearls*. We waited in the car until it was over, then went into the Coliseum to check out the cars. Man, what a crowd! It was lucky Matty and I weren't interested in the new models. You couldn't even get close. We headed for the corner of the huge hall where the '30's and early '40's cars were. It was still crowded, but back there, at least you could see without waiting in line to get close.

That's where we saw it. A 1936 model Cord phaeton. It was the last year they were made. Man, that car was something else! You can look at it today, and the styling and detail make Detroit stuff look like garbage. Over forty years ago, they had built an automatic gear shifter and a supercharger into the Cord. And it had front-wheel drive thirty years before the first Olds Toronado and Caddy Eldo. Face it, back then they made cars, music, almost everything better. Or maybe it's just me. Like, if you've ever had a feeling that you really didn't belong to your own time, you probably have some period in history you think you'd have done better. For me, it's the '40's. Yeah, I know it wasn't really what you'd call a happy time. There was World War II going on, and things were grim, at first. In the first two years of the war, we almost lost to the Nazis and Japanese. And for the first time, a war really affected the American people at home, beyond losing someone in battle. Gas, tires, even food and coffee, were rationed. You couldn't buy those things without rationing coupons. Cars had windshield stickers with letters on them to show how much gasoline you were allowed to buy. The higher the letter in the alphabet you had, the more gas you could get. An "A" card was the lowest, and a card marked "X" was the best. I found that out from Harry. But even he didn't remember it too well. He was only thirteen when the war ended. But for all of it being wartime, at least you could tell who the good guys and the bad guys were. Not like now, when it seems that we Americans are always the bad guys.

Matty was happy as a pig in swill. He's nuts about cars, and the older the better. That's how we got to be such good buddies. He's crazy about the '40's, too. He was always interested in the cars, and I got him going on the music. Started out when Mr. Davis assigned the marching band the *Saint Louis Blues March*. I already knew that the Glenn Miller Band had played this arrangement when Miller went into the army during World War II. When I saw how much Matty dug it at practice, we got to talking.

It ended up with Matty coming home with me and listening to my collection of big band reissues. Since that time, we've been tight. We had some problems for a time with the salt-pepper thing. My mom looked at me funny when I brought Matty home. Black and white don't mix much in Branford outside of school. Matty's folks weren't too tickled, either. Matty's mom was still alive then. But after a while, our folks got used to it. So did the kids in Branford. But for all the acceptance, we still don't double-date unless Matty has set it up with a black chick in advance.

When we first got to be friends, we tried a few times cruising in Matty's Chevy. But we'd scare off most white chicks when they saw Matty, and cruising over in Thornton, which is a mostly black town near Branford, isn't too healthy. Thornton is so tough, Matty doesn't like to go there.

And one time, when we went to a rock concert at the Felt Forum in Manhattan with two white chicks, we nearly got wiped out by a bunch of black dudes who didn't care for seeing us all together. It's really sad. The race thing doesn't matter to either me or Matty, but it seems people just can't leave other people alone. If either Matty's folks or mine heard some of the things we say to each other, kidding about the black-white relationship, they'd take turns whamming on us. Each set of parents for a different reason.

For the most part, the only places we go where we don't draw a second glance is at jazz clubs and concerts. Even that seems to be changing. You see fewer and fewer mixed jazz and rock groups. Music, which used to bring people together, seems to be breaking down, too. It wasn't that way in the '40's, but now . . .

We finished up at the Coliseum about eight o'clock. We could have hung around looking at the old cars, but we were both getting hungry. I had the money from Harry, so we had dinner on me. We hit a Sirloin Sid's, where I know they don't check I.D.'s too close, and had a couple of steaks and maybe a little too much red wine. They give you all you can drink there, in pitchers. And it wasn't like we were so underage. Matty will be eighteen in just three weeks. I make it legal a month after Matty. We're both tall and look a little older than we are, so most places we get drinks, no sweat. I think it's been easier since Matty grew the moustache. It isn't much of a brush, as Matty says, but it does the job.

When we drove back to Branford, listening to a tape of the Benny Goodman Quartet, Matty drove right past my turnoff. I called his attention to it.

"I know," he said, "but it's about the same time as you took that walk last night. I want to go out to the cemetery and have a look."

I was so wrapped up in Harry pulling his cheap trick earlier that I'd almost forgotten about it. But I knew Mom would be bombed when I got home. She always does that when I spend time with Harry. I wasn't anxious for another scene today, so I went along with Matty.

The cemetery gate wasn't locked. It never is. After all,

who's going to steal anything in there? We didn't park on
25-A. That could have drawn a curious patrol car. We
drove inside. Matty remembered the general area. He'd
scouted it two days before for a place to stash the beer.
Once we got to the section where Abner Pew's stone
was, he parked and killed the lights. We took a flashlight
from the glove compartment and got out to look around.

We'd been poking through the tightly spaced stones
for a few minutes. I was getting ready to quit. It had
been so easy to find last night, too. I was about to tell
Matty I'd had it, when this incredible deep bass voice
said, "Who be ye that seek the Keeper of the Gate?
Stand and be seen!"

The voice was bad enough. Matty was holding the
flash, and we both turned simultaneously, like somebody
had kicked us from behind at the same time. I was glad
Matty held the light. I would have dropped it and run.
Maybe he would have, too, but he told me later he was
too scared to move. I wouldn't have blamed him. Because there, in the beam of the flash, was one of the
biggest black men I've ever seen. He was easy six-five
and about three hundred pounds. He was wearing a
Colonial outfit, like the guy I'd seen at the Branford
Inne. But he wasn't in shirt-sleeves. He wore a three-
cornered hat and a big heavy coat. Around his waist was
a thick, wide, leather belt. In it were two old-fashioned
pistols. The sabre that should have been in the empty
scabbard that hung from the belt was in his right hand.
He was so big, it looked like a toy in that huge paw of his.
He didn't look like he was too glad to see us.

"Be ye deef?" he thundered. "Who seeks the Gatekeeper?"

Then, sabre in hand, he rushed at us!

3

Ghost of a Chance

I nearly went through the ground. Matty and I both stood there for a second. It was all the big man needed. He was right on top of us, quick as a cat, for all his size. The big blade of the sabre began to descend. I tensed up, and it must have looked like I was trying to pull my head inside me like a turtle. The blade whistled down and then . . . stopped dead, less than an inch from my scalp. I swear I felt it on my hair, which I was sure was standing up on end.

"Hold, now," he growled. "Ye aren't but a couple of lads." He looked closer at Matty. "A young squire and servant from the look of ye. What brings ye here to seek the Gatekeeper?"

"The Gatekeeper?" I asked like a dodo. "What's that?"

The big man laughed. The laugh started at about D below middle C on the scale, and I know it sounds hard, but got even deeper.

"Not what, young squire," he laughed, "*who* is the

23

question. You are speaking to him. I be Abner Pew, freeman, soldier, poet, musician and Keeper of the Gate. Who be ye?"

"I be . . .er, I'm Richie Gilroy. This is my friend, Matty Owen."

Abner Pew took a long, hard look at Matty. Matty swallowed hard and said, "Pleased to meet you, Mr. Pew."

I have to hand it to Matty. He kept his cool. When he gave Abner Pew the how-do-you-do, he even put out his hand. I don't know if Matty did it on purpose, but you can't shake someone's hand if you have a sabre in yours. Pew sheathed the big blade and grasped Matty's outstretched hand.

"Ye may call me Abner, lad," he said. Then he looked again at me and back to Matty. "The young squire calls you his friend. Then ye must be a freeman, like myself. S'truth?"

Matty relaxed visibly. I knew the look. Once Matty has a scene figured out, he drops his shoulders; it's an un-tensing move. I could even tell by the tone of his voice when he said to the big black man, "Free as a bird." He smiled.

Pew pushed his hat back on his head and walked over and sat down on his own tombstone. He pulled out a clay pipe and filled it with dark, evil-looking tobacco. He took a flint and a piece of steel from a pouch at his belt, and after a few scrapes, had a little red coal glowing in the bowl of his pipe. As he moved into the path of the flashlight beam, I noticed a large, dark stain on the back of his coat, right between the shoulder blades.

When he opened his coat to sit down, my stomach turned over. There was an equally large stain on his white shirt front. It was old and dried, but there's no mistaking the look and color if you've ever had a wound bandaged. It was blood, all right. Pew smiled when he saw me staring at it. "I see you're interested in m'wound, young squire," he said. "It doesn't pain me, if that's what ye be thinking. Haven't thought of it meself in many years. . . . Hold a minute! Can ye shine the lantern on yerself a bit?"

Matty flashed the light off of Abner Pew and onto me. Pew got up and came closer.

"Ah! It is you. The lad I let through the Gate by mistake last night. It was God's good graces that saved ye, young squire. Had ye not returned when ye did, I couldn't have fetched ye, for I can't enter the Gate meself. I'm only the Keeper. Ye were close as a heart's beat to being lost forever."

I really didn't know what Abner Pew was talking about. I knew now that he had something to do with me being in Old Branford, but he kept on talking as though I should have known what the connection was. I didn't ask him to explain. You don't interrupt a guy that size when he's talking, even if he isn't armed to the teeth the way Abner Pew was. Pew turned his attention to Matty again. He walked around Matty like he was some new kind of bug that had turned up.

"So ye be a freeman?" he said slowly. "From the look of ye, a quadroon to begin with. Your natural father was no African, lad. Was it he who freed ye?"

It sunk in on me what Abner was talking about. Nowadays, we don't think a lot about what shade of black a black man is. But in Pew's time, most blacks in this country hadn't been born here. Their African blood hadn't been thinned out. Pew himself, for instance. He was extremely dark. He thought that because Matty isn't particularly dark skinned, that he was some slave owner's illegitimate son by a slave mother. Pew didn't wait for Matty's answer to his question about Matty's father. He sat down again and began to talk, more to himself it seemed.

"Ah, ye had it lucky, er, Matthew, is it?"

"Yes, Abner," said Matty in a small voice.

"Well, I had no such good fortune myself. Came here with Blackbirders when I was only eight years old. Traveled with my mother in the hold. I'll never forget it. It was then I saw that whore son, Branford, for the first time."

"Would that be Nathaniel Branford?" I asked.

You'd have thought I'd insulted Pew and all his ancestors. The big man's face grew even darker. He looked like some huge thundercloud about to break into a storm. One with a lot of lightning.

"Be there another?" he roared. "Were there ten thousand, I'd gladly spend my last drop of blood to kill them all. Scum! All of Branford and Branford's get are scum. A plague on them all!"

Pew got up and put his hand on the hilt of the sabre again. I don't mind saying it made me nervous. I glanced over at Matty. He looked ready to pick up and run, too. But Pew was on his feet now, and stalking around his tombstone like a great predatory animal. He saw me edge closer to Matty. I mean, if Matty was going to cut and run, I wanted to be with him. First, just for company. Second, although there was some moonlight, Matty had the flashlight. As if he knew my thoughts, Pew cut in, "Move if ye dare! But ye'll not go until ye hear the tale of Abner Pew. Thrice free, twice diddled of his birthright by that bastard Branford!"

Matty and I both sat down. Seeing we weren't going to split, Pew took his hand off the sabre and, not taking his eyes off us, told this tale:

"I was born in Africa, the second son of the favorite wife of a prince. We were raided by Berbers from the north of Africa. We knew nothing of modern warfare. Not a man in my tribe had so much as seen a flintlock.

We fought with the courage of lions, but spears against powder and shot must ever face defeat. My father was slain and my mother and I taken captive.

"We were marched in chains to the West Coast of Africa, where we were sold to an American slave trader, bound for the New World. When we came to Charleston, in the Carolinas, I was separated from my mother. She was sold, and I remained. I can still see the face of the man who ran the slave auction that day, may his soul burn in Hell forever. It was Nathaniel Branford!"

"I can't blame you for hating him, Abner," said Matty.

"Were that all!" growled Pew. "For that alone, I would part his feculent head from his putrid carcass. But nay, there's more. Much more!

"I was sold to Moses Pew, a minister of the Gospel. He was a kind old gentleman. He raised me more as his son than as his body servant. From Moses Pew, I learned the white man's languages: English, French, Latin, Greek, and Hebrew. I learned proper manner of dress and address. As the minister was an old man, and none too strong, he had me learn the use of arms from some military acquaintances of his, for he needed protection.

"Though my aptitude for Greek and Hebrew was lacking, when it came to the use of arms, my warrior blood came to the fore. I became adept at sabre and épée, lance and musket. Though no man from my tribe had ever sat a horse, the saddle was as natural to me as eating. Major Quentin, my teacher, told me that in another day I should have been like Shakespeare's Othello, a great general and leader of men and nations.

"But all my skill in the martial arts was to no avail in saving the life of my protector, Moses Pew. As I attained young manhood, I thought of him ever as protector, not master, you see. For he had been more father to me than my own, whose memory had long dimmed. I was desolated when he died of the smallpox. I wept for him, and have shed no tears but those of rage since that day. But my woes had just begun.

"The magistrate in charge of seeing to Moses Pew's estate was that swine, Branford. I knew full well Moses Pew had made me a freeman in his will. Had I not scribed it myself when, from age, Reverend Pew's hand had faltered? But protest as I might, it was futile in the face of Branford's schemes and the bribes he had taken from Moses Pew's only heir, a distant cousin. I was denied my freedom, and again sold into slavery. And yet again, by that cur, Branford!"

Matty whistled tonelessly and said, "Abner, I'd say you had some run of hard luck, for one man."

The huge man didn't get Matty's drift. He took it the way it was said. He nodded in agreement, gravely, then went on, "Indeed, I, too, considered that it were the Fates, for the Fates have ever governed the lives of soldiers. But at that time, I did not consider it either Fates or God's will, though had it been God's will, I should still have endured the trials of Job smiling and singing God's praises. Had but that God offered me the neck of Branford between these hands!"

Abner Pew held up two paws the size of dinner plates. I shuddered at the thought of what it might feel like, those hands around my neck.

"But it was not to be," went on Abner Pew. "I was carted off to Virginia, supposedly to become a house servant for a wealthy planter. I recall his name not, for I never served him. On the way, a careless overseer and a dark night helped me gain the freedom rightfully mine."

Abner Pew paused and glanced up at the half-moon in the sky. In profile, his features were a little softer. An almost sweet and dreamy look came over his face. He looked like a picture of a black saint, peaceful, serene.

"Unfortunately," he went on in a somewhat distant tone, "that same careless overseer somehow contrived to break his neck that same dark night . . ." He opened his hands in a gentle gesture. "Naturally, Abner Pew being the only slave absent from the list in the morning, poor Abner was accused of murder."

I looked at those hands, so huge, yet gentle in repose. With a shudder, I realized that they could have snapped a neck like a matchstick. In a flash, I knew how that overseer had managed to "break his neck." Pew wasn't fooling Matty a bit about the overseer's "accident," either.

"Isn't it terrible the way some folks talk?" put in Matty, smiling.

This time, Abner Pew didn't mistake Matty's meaning. He gave Matty a horrid, wolfish grin and said, "Scandalous. As a quadroon, you can perceive my difficult situation, I'm certain. I fled the country to Louisiana, where my color posed fewer obstacles, and my French was appreciated. From there to Europe and on to service for so many beys, pashas, and sultans that they grow as one in my memory—short, fat little men who smelled of perfume and loved the sounds of pain inflicted by man upon men.

"But no matter how high I rose in the service of sultans (and I once commanded a brigade), I never renounced my claim to revenge on the cursed Branford. And one day, when I had grown rich enough, and with papers of citizenship bearing the great seal of the Sultan of Turkey himself, I set off for the Carolinas to find Branford. But the serpent had fled in disgrace. As a magistrate, he had taken one bribe too many.

"It consumed the better part of a year to find the trail of his cloven hoof. Finally, I found him. He was in command of a raggle-taggle company of a rural militia. No man in it, from commander down, would have been fit to lick the boots of a true soldier. It was no accident that the King's men trounced them as they did.

"The day I arrived at Mills Hostel, on Long Island, in New York, Branford, the ninny, had allowed the King's troops to come upon his entire company whilst at drill in the field! The village common was obscured from view by the powder smoke, but as it drifted in the morning breeze, I saw the face of my enemy, my oppressor, my curse: Branford!

"With a scream of rage, I drew my blade and flew at him. No sooner had I the wretch within the reach of my sword's point, when I was struck mortally from behind by a British musket ball. Not yet quite dead, I was dragged away with the other wounded in the course of Branford's retreat. Nor was I yet dead when we reached safety from British fire. I had to endure the ultimate humility of that pustule Branford recognizing me after many years. In my helpless condition, I bore the further indignity of Branford forgiving me for the crime of taking my rightful freedom. A reward for coming between the rogue and a British ball. I had accidentally saved his life! Even in death, I was not spared the curse of this man. Through eternity, I must see his name on my poor gravestone. Can you now conceive of the hatred I bear him?"

Matty stood up. He walked over to Abner Pew and rested his hand on his great shoulder. "Conceive of it? Brother, if he wasn't almost two hundred years dead, I'd help you go get him!" Matty eyed Abner Pew. "Not that I think you'd need any help, bro. I'm sure you could handle it just fine."

"But, Abner," I asked, "what has all this to do with what you said about gates and being a gatekeeper? We came in through the cemetery gate. But your grave is way back here."

Abner Pew knocked out the ash from his pipe, then stood up and stretched. Now, I'm over six feet tall and weigh about 170 pounds, but I want to tell you it was a humbling sight. He seemed to almost blot out the moon when he stood.

"I would beg your pardons. Many years have elapsed since I last spoke to one who would enter the Gate. I grow lonely with no companion save my hatred of a memory. Yes, I keep the Gate. It lies less than a hand-span from where you stand, Matthew."

Matty turned around full circle with the flashlight in his hand. "I sure don't see anything that looks like a gate, Abner."

"It is there, for all of that," said Pew, "though not a gate of the sort you might think. It is the reason ye see me before you. For in death, as in life, the Fates still pursue me. The site of my grave sits directly upon a mistake in Time itself, a passageway to all that has gone before. There are such places on this planet where the forces of Time come together. And if one knows the proper ritual, he may pass from Future to Past as easily as one may enter side rooms from the great hall of a manor house.

"The final joke of the Fates placed me here. Though a freeman, and albeit accidentally a hero, I was still a black man and so was buried in a part of this cemetery unused by whites. I found no freedom, even in death. For this aperture in Time has tangled my soul as surely as a fish taken in a seine. I remain here, in neither Heaven nor Hell, in death as in life, between two worlds and belonging to neither.

"When a short time before my death, I returned to my native land in Africa, I found myself too much a product of my years with the white man. I was not a true member of my people's culture any longer, nor was I accepted by the white man as a full member of his society. Perhaps it is only meet that I have become the guardian of this Gate."

"You mean you just took it on yourself to guard it?"

"Nay, young squire. I was commissioned to do so by powers I be not free to discuss. As a good soldier, I know but what I need know, the better to carry out my duties. In like manner, I know this is but one of several Gates to the Past. but I know not where they be, nor the names of their Keepers."

"Wait a minute," said Matty. "You mean there are a whole bunch of these whatzits, holes in Time?"

Pew sat down again. He checked his pipe and, satisfied it was empty, returned it to his greatcoat.

"Aye, though not easily found. And each Gate has a guardian to ensure that no stranger unwittingly stumbles through. But betimes, mistakes do occur. Young Master Richard, for example. I saw him too late. I was off in another part of this graveyard, attending to a matter of natural urgency. (I always do so in one place—the grave of the accursed Branford.) I espied him at the Gate entrance, and were too distant to hail him. As I watched, he performed the ritual necessary to enter the Gate. He paced two steps forward from the foot of my grave, then turned and strode away . . ."

"That's when I saw my wallet and went to get it!" I put in.

"That may well be," continued Pew, "but the ritual itself is not easily performed unless already known. When the ritual was devised, it were thought that no man would purposefully tread upon a stranger's grave. This alone prevents most accidental entries through the Gate."

"It would have stopped me, too. But I wanted to get my wallet," I said.

"Ah. Ye do still observe the sanctity of the grave in

this time, then," said Abner Pew. "And from where I stood, I could not see whether ye had a key in your possession. I assumed ye were a True Traveler in Time, by grace of your performance of the rite. And as ye were dressed in the garb of a Continental soldier, I assumed your destination in Time to be of that era. So I sent ye to the year necessary."

"But how did I get back?" I asked in wonder.

"Ye returned by repeating the ritual. True, it were by coincidence ye did it. But the Gate treats accidents and purposeful entries as one. It . . ." Pew fell silent for a moment. He gave Matty and me a hard look, then continued, "I know not if I be doing the proper thing now. For to explain how it came about may be telling more than I be allowed," he said. "But as ye have already done the deed, I opine that it would do no harm."

Pew shifted his position and untied the lace scarf he wore at his throat. He scratched behind his left ear, then said, "This portal into Time were discovered many years hence, far in your Future. The men who found it know more of its workings than poor Abner Pew, for I found it only when accidentally buried in an undesirable part of this graveyard. And though I know little of how it truly functions, I do know the procedures for its operation. For instance, the Gate has safeguards other than the ritual. A True Traveler in Time carries with him one or two of these keys . . ."

Pew reached down to the wide belt that kept his greatcoat closed and came up with two big iron keys, each about ten inches long.

"They serve as both guides and identification. When a True Traveler nears a Gate, the key grows warm and in the darkness, even glows with a spirit-like light. Carrying these keys also identifies the True Traveler to each Gatekeeper."

"But Abner," I objected, "I didn't have a key."

"True. But I had no way of knowing that. As I say, ye were distant from me . . ."

"But I also got back to my own time," I said.

"Another of the Gate's safeguards," rumbled Pew. "Once a Gate is entered, the traveler, be he a True Traveler, or a traveler by happenstance, like yourself, may return by the same Gate to his own Time. But this be only if he makes his return journey within an hour's time. After he has remained on the other side of the Gate for more than an hour's span, he becomes of the Time he visits, and he may never return again, save by a Gate to the Future. This portal I guard is a Gate to the Past."

I swallowed hard, thinking of how close I'd come to being stuck in Old Branford for the rest of my life.

"You mean to tell me that if I hadn't come right back, I'd still be there?"

Pew nodded gravely. "There have been such cases. I have been told of one man in Italy, many years in your Past. He lived a long, rewarding life, for he had knowledge of many future artifacts and was in addition an accomplished painter and sculptor. I am told that some of his works are still much prized in your day, young Master Richard."

Matty whistled tonelessly. Then he leaned over close to me and whispered, "Richie, I think he's talking about Leonardo da Vinci."

"Aye, that be his name," said Pew, who I guess had sharper ears than Matty thought. "Though he were never able to return to his own time, he lived well and long."

I'd seen a few TV shows about Da Vinci. What Abner Pew said made a lot of sense. There was Leonardo from our own time, drawing plans for tanks, submarines and helicopters back then. I'd wondered where he could have gotten such ideas. Now I knew. A germ of an idea was forming in my mind. It must have occurred to Matty at the same time. He spoke up and asked Abner Pew the same thing I was going to ask.

"Can we see how it works, Abner?" asked Matty. "Just once? We won't stay. Can you send us back in Time, just for a few seconds?"

Abner Pew stroked the side of his chin, as though feeling for whiskers that would never grow again.

"Aye, I can do that, Matthew," said Pew. "I would do ye that favor, for ye have heard my tale with sympathetic ears, and ye be partly of my race." Pew stood up. "Walk here, Matthew. You, too, young squire."

I went over to the spot Pew indicated, directly at the foot of his grave.

"Now," said Pew, "face my headstone. Walk two paces, turn, then walk away as toward the entrance to this grave-yard . . ." Both Matty and I started doing exactly what Abner Pew said.

"Hold!" he snapped. "Do not begin the process until you have learnt it all. To return, ye must repeat the procedure. Once ye enter the Gate, I cannot guide you, for I must remain here at the entryway to the Gate. Have ye in mind exactly what ye must do?"

We repeated the drill word for word to Pew until he was satisfied that we knew how it worked. Pew made a gesture, like "After you," and we stepped through the Gate.

I didn't feel anything different, except for a momentary chill, as though somebody had walked over my grave. I looked around and sure enough, Abner Pew had vanished! As if for assurance, I put my hand on Matty's shoulder.

"Where do you think we are, Matty?"

"Not where, but when," he said. "I don't know. Pew didn't say when-to he was sending us."

We looked around us. The stars were brighter than I'd ever seen them. The writing on Abner Pew's gravestone looked sharper and newer, but that was it.

"Not very impressive," I thought aloud.

"Well, what do you expect?" asked Matty. "Now or a hundred years ago, there wouldn't be much happening in a graveyard at this hour, anyway. As far as I can see, the sky's a little clearer. That'd be because there wasn't so much air pollution long ago. But this could just as easy be last Friday as last century."

"Guess you're right, babe," I said. "It is kind of a letdown, isn't it?"

We went through the drill of facing the stone, turning, and felt the same goose bump feeling again. Abner Pew was waiting for us.

"Well, lads," he said. "How did ye enjoy the last century? I sent ye to 1878."

"Tell you the truth, Abner," said Matty, "it wasn't too different from now. After all, a graveyard at night's a graveyard at night. See one, you've seen 'em all."

"True, true," said Pew solemnly. "Ye could have gone into the village. Ye had the time."

"How long were we gone, Abner?" I asked.

"I noticed not," said Pew, "for it matters not. When a traveler passes through the Gate and returns within an hour's time, he returns to the same instant in Time at which he departed. Ye were gone for an eye blink and returned here in the same span of time."

"As though we were never gone," said Matty.

"Exactly so," said Pew. "But had ye remained past the hour's grace, I should have noticed your absence. For, past the hour's grace, Time would again begin to flow here."

"Wait a minute, Abner," I said. "What about those other travelers you mentioned? They're gone for more than an hour. Aren't they missed back in their own time?"

"Not the True Traveler," replied Pew. "These folk return not by the Gate by which they enter. As I told ye, there be many such Gates to Future and Past. If the True Traveler journeys in the Past, he returns by the Future Gate. If he journeys into the Future, he returns by the Past Gate. In each case, he instructs the Gate-keeper to return him to the exact moment he departed. Thus, he were never gone at all to the folk of his Time."

"And this Gate works only to the Past?" asked Matty.

"Save for the hour's grace I told ye of," said Pew.

I wasn't sure I understood it all, but an excitement was building inside me. The germ of the idea was beginning to grow stronger. I didn't want to discuss it in front of Abner Pew. I wasn't even sure I wanted to say it aloud to Matty. Not until I was sure.

Matty and I swore to Pew that we wouldn't tell anything about the Gate or Pew himself to anyone else. It was an easy promise. After all, who'd have believed us? Tell someone a tale like that, and you'd end up in a rubber room at the local loony bin. We promised, too, that we'd come to see Pew once in a while, so he'd have somebody to talk to.

As we left the graveyard, I glanced back. Pew was a great shadowy bulk, still sitting on his tombstone in the half moonlight. Just as the Chevy began to roll, I saw him striking flint and steel together to light another pipe. I wondered absently how the tobacco in his pouch had lasted for all these years. Neither Matty nor I said anything until we were well along 25-A headed for Branford. It was I who broke the silence.

"Matty, I want to go back in Time."

He kept driving, and after a few minutes he said, "Where or when in Time, Richie?"

"You don't know?" I said in disbelief. "I want to go back to the '40's. I want to hear all those great sounds live, not on bad recordings. Will you go with me, Matty?"

"I'll think about it," he said.

When Matty dropped me off at home, Mom was passed out on the sofa. The channel she'd been watching had gone off the air. The screen was a bluish blank, and the set was making a hissing sound. I turned it off and put a blanket over Mom. She stirred a bit when I kissed her cheek and turned out the light in the living room.

Once in my own bed, I couldn't sleep. I kept thinking of how it would be to actually hear and see Glenn Miller or Louis Armstrong. I think it was then that I truly made up my mind.

4

Swingin' on the Old Time Gate

It wasn't until four weeks later that Matty and I stood once again at the foot of Abner Pew's grave. We were ready to go, even to the way we were dressed. It had taken some time, and a lot of bad changes had gone down by then, too.

I guess the biggest change was with Matty. Last week, when he'd turned eighteen, we'd partied pretty hard. After the regular party at Matty's house, he and I had bounced around some jazz places in Manhattan. You can still hear traditional jazz and swing played in New York City nowadays, if you know where to go. We'd both gotten pretty bombed in the process. So when Matty parked the Chevy on his father's front lawn instead of in the garage, all hell broke loose.

There had been an argument between Matty and his dad that nearly ended up in a fistfight. I got between them, and with the help of Matty's sister, Loretta, had cooled them both out before it got too hairy. But the upshot of the whole mess was that Matty moved out of his father's house.

See, Matty's argument had been that if he was eighteen, he was his own man and didn't have to answer to anyone. His dad figured that as long as Matty was under his roof, Matty would do as he was told. Matty said OK, and packed a bag. He'd been living in our spare bedroom ever since.

The first night Matty stayed over at my house, we'd discussed the possibility of going backwards in time.

"Richie, you're out of your tree!" Matty had said. "If we go through that Gate and go into Manhattan, we'll never be able to come back. You heard what Pew said, that after an hour, we'd be stuck there for good. And it takes easy an hour just to get into New York from here. God only knows how long it took in . . . what was the date you wanted to go to?"

"First weekend in February, 1942," I answered.

"Yeah, whatever. By the time we get there, our hour will be up, and we'll have to spend the rest of our lives from 1942 on. Do you realize that by the time we get back to 1976, we'll both be over fifty years old?"

"Matty, I told you. That's if we can't get to the Future Gate. If we can find the Future Gate, we can come back before we left, if we want. Nobody would even know we'd been gone."

"Come to think of it," said Matty ruefully, "I don't know if either one of us would be missed. They might miss us at graduation exercises, but face it, where are we going after the end of this month, anyway?"

Matty was talking about another bad thing that had happened. I'd failed the entrance exam to the Juilliard School of Music the week before. My sight reading has always been crappy outside of bass clef. I'd thought that the exam would consist of me playing an audition on either tuba or string bass. But for some strange reason, they want you to know it all at Juilliard. I'm used to bass clef, which is the way all music for bass instruments is notated. At the exam, they'd thrown a lot of treble clef at me and expected me to sight-read it. I was OK on harmony, and I knew that my audition piece on string bass was good. But I got all screwed up with the ledger lines in treble clef and couldn't read the music too well. After all, I'm no piccolo player. Anyway, I flunked.

Matty had passed with flying colors, but it didn't do him any good. Unless he made peace with his dad, there wouldn't be any tuition money so he could go to Juilliard. We were both kind of at a dead end. And graduation was just a few weeks away.

So we started playing "What if?" with the idea of going back in Time through Abner Pew's Gate. I think I took it more seriously than Matty. I went into New York City a bunch of times and researched the old copies of newspapers and magazines at the library on 42nd Street. I wrote down who was playing where, and what was going on in New York at the time. The whole enchilada. By the time I told Matty I was ready, I think I knew the week in question cold enough to take a test on the subject.

For instance, in February, 1942, Mayor La Guardia of New York was promising the city that he'd hold the five-cent fare on subways and trolley cars firm until at least September. Some laugh! I'd seen the current mayor of New York say the same thing about the fifty-cent fare on TV just the night before. Coffee and Coke cost a nickel, same as phone calls at pay stations. A good dinner at any of the better places cost no more than $3.95. And if you went to the Automat, you could get a good meal for under fifty cents!

I'd even rummaged through thrift shops and old clothes stores and found us outfits to wear. Knowing that paper money printed in the 1970's would pose a problem, I raided the coin collection I'd had since I was ten years old. Harry had helped me with it, at first. I had a collection of silver dollars, sixty-five of them from before 1942. Figuring what things cost back then, I didn't see any problems about getting along for a week or even two, if we watched the money carefully.

Matty and I drilled on our World War II history until names were shooting out of our ears. Some of it was easy. Like, most folks know that in 1942, Hitler was boss of Germany and the Emperor Hirohito and his number one man, Tojo, ran Japan. Mussolini was dictator of Italy, Winston Churchill was Prime Minister of England, Franklin D. Roosevelt was President of the United States. Any school kid with a passing grade in history can tell you that. But what about who was Vice-president? Who commanded the Free French Army? Who was Secretary of State? It's not so easy, you see.

Things were different in a lot of other ways, too. There were no ball-point pens. They weren't invented yet. No frozen foods, no TV. Hardly any man-made fibers like Orlon, Dacron, Nylon, or polyesters. Portable radios were the size of shoe boxes and weighed a ton. No transistors. I knew when I looked over what I should have known, there was no way I could memorize it all. But I knew I could learn enough to get by for a week or two, and that's all I thought I needed.

But a time comes when all preparations made can't bring you any further. I felt it was time to give it a try. But when I asked Matty if he was ready, all he said was, "Yeah, I guess so, Richie."

"What do you mean, 'I guess so'?" I said impatiently. "If you weren't serious about all this, why have you been going through the motions, all the research and work we've done?"

Matty looked away for a minute, then said, "Tell you the truth, man. I wasn't all that sure that you were really going to do it. And I figured it wasn't lost time. I'm just as interested in the '40's as you are. And it was fun getting the clothes and trying them on, like a game, y'know? But really doing it, that's something else . . ."

"What's the matter?" I asked, regretting it even as I said it. "Scared?"

Matty stood up, but he didn't get mad, like I thought he would. He walked around the room, then came back to his chair and looked me straight in the eye.

"Yeah, I'm scared, Richie," he said, "and I think if you had any sense, you'd be scared, too. Face it, babe. I love you like a brother, but you've got some kind of fantasy about the '40's. You think it'll be all great sounds and a good time. But I tell you this. If we get into trouble, nobody's gonna bail us out but us. I worry about that, but it isn't what bothers me most."

"What does, then?" I asked.

"It's this one-way Gate in Time business. Don't you see that if we don't like it back then, it's just tough. We *can't* get back!"

"We can always find the Future Gate," I said, sounding surer than I really was.

"But what if we can't?" said Matty exasperatedly. "Will you admit that it is a big chance we're taking?"

"What isn't a chance in life?" I came back. "I'll tell you this. I'm going alone or with you. But believe it, I'm going."

The tension between us was almost thick enough to see. Then Matty smiled and stuck out his hand. "You're on, bro."

Matty went out to the cemetery a few times alone to see Abner Pew. He'd told me that he could probably get tighter with Pew, as one black man to another, if I wasn't along. He told me that the big man had been touched when Matty brought him some imported pipe tobacco. But I don't think it was so much the tobacco that got us through to Abner. The night we got ready to jump off, I also brought along a fifth of 151 proof rum from our liquor cabinet. When I handed it to him, he broke out in a grin that looked like it would split his face. I noticed at the time he had surprisingly small teeth for a man his size.

"Bless ye, young squire," he said. "It's been three lifetimes since I've had so much as a dram of rum."

He tilted the bottle to his lips and then began to worry at the screw cap with his teeth. I wondered at first what he was doing. Then I realized that Abner had never seen a screw-top bottle before. He was trying to pull out the cork with his teeth, like you see in movies. I showed him how it worked.

"Unnecessary," he said, tossing the screw cap over his shoulder. He put the opened bottle to his lips and pointed it at the sky. In less than a gulg or two, he'd drained half the bottle.

"Hey!" said Matty, "be careful, Abner. That stuff's 151 proof."

Abner Pew wiped his lips with a lace handkerchief he produced from his coatsleeve, exhaled mightily, and said, "I know not what proof be, but this be fair rum. Tastes like a good Demerara."

It was my turn to pull a blank. I didn't know that Demerara is a kind of rum. Abner took another pull from the jug and another quarter of it disappeared. He sat down on his grave plot and leaned back against his headstone. Pew took off his three-cornered hat and scaled it across a nearby monument. He looked up at the night sky and began to sing softly in a voice so deep it sounded like a mourning marine diesel engine.

> *"Man, man, man is for the woman made,*
> *And the woman for the man . . ."*

Matty took me aside. "Listen, Richie, I don't know how smart it was to bring the rum. If this dude gets wrecked, he could hurt us both, just playing around."

> *"Be she wanton, be she maid,*
> *Be she well or ill arrayed . . ."*

"Well, it seemed like a good idea at the time," I whispered. "If he's mellowed out, it'll be easier talking him into letting us go through."

"Great," said Matty. "But this guy hasn't had a taste in over two hundred years. He'll be gonezo in a few more slugs." Pew was picking up volume now.

> *"Queen, slut or harridan,*
> *Man, man, man is for the woman made,*
> *And the woman for the man!"*

By the time he reached the end of the verse, Pew was in full cry. His voice seemed to shake the ground. He took another slug from the bottle of rum and regarded Matty and me from where he sat on his own grave.

"Ah, ye be good lads," he rumbled. "And this be the fairest rum to pass me lips in many a year." He held the bottle up to Matty's flashlight beam and examined the label. "Tell me, young Richard," he said. "Who be this man, Don Q?"

I realized in a flash. He saw the brand name on the jug, and he thought that the stuff was actually made by some guy called Don Q. I wasn't about to go into the way booze is merchandized in the twentieth century. So I said, "A distiller, Abner."

"A man of rare taste," said Pew. "I should like to make his acquaintance one day. Any man who can make a rum like this has poetry in his soul. *'As the spur is to the jade, as the scepter to be swayed, as for digging is the spade . . .'*" he caroled.

"Abner," cut in Matty.

" *'So man, man, man is for the woman made,'* " roared Pew.

"Abner!" hollered Matty. But no good. Pew wasn't going to be denied the big ending to his tune. He stood up, stretched both his arms out and thundered to the gravestones and trees, " '*And the wo-oh-man forrr the mannn!*' " Then he sat down again, and closed his eyes and began to snore like a buzz saw in heat.

"Great," said Matty. "He's zonked. C'mon, Rich. Let's forget the whole thing. He's gone for the night."

Just as Matty said that, Pew stirred again and looked around him. He gave a start when he saw Matty and me, then once it sank in on him who we were, he gave us a bleary smile.

"Ah, young friends, ye haven't left, then. Good. Tell me, ye be musicians. Do you know Purcell's *Indian Queen?*" He began to sing again.

> "*If love's a sweet passion,*
> *Why does it torment? . . .*"

"Mr. Pew!" hollered Matty.

Abner stopped short. "Yes, Matthew?" he asked. "What service can I do ye? For a bottle of nectar such as this, I'd grant any boon. What would ye know? The mysteries of the stars? I have studied them. Would ye speak of Newton's logic? Ask, but ask . . ."

"We want to go through the Gate, Abner," I spoke up. "We want to go back to February of 1942."

Pew ran his fingers through his hair and shook his head, as though to clear it of the rum fumes. But in the next minute, he took another monster swig from what was left of the rum. He'd put away nearly a quart of 151 proof rum in less than fifteen minutes! His eyes were at half mast, and it looked like he was about to pass out, so I talked fast, "Really, Abner, we do. I've planned it all out, and I know this time in history. I have money, our clothes are right. I know where we want to go and for how long. Just for a week, maybe two."

"Ye could not return to this time by this Gate," said Pew fuzzily.

"We'll find the Future Gate," I said, sounding surer than I was. Pew sat up and cleared momentarily.

"Ye'd never find it. Ye knew not for what ye are searching," he said, then started to drift out of focus again. He reached down to his belt and took off the iron key ring. He slipped one of the big keys off and handed it to me. "This be the Key to the Future Gate," he mumbled. "Take it and Godspeed. Ye will find the Future Gate where the compass needle spins, and the horizon changes place with the sea. The Key will lead ye. It glows and grows warm when near its Gate. I have kept this key all the years against the possible time I might have need of it . . ."

"But I thought you couldn't even go through the Gate . . ." I began.

He waved me into silence. "I have told ye what can be comprehended by one of your Time, young squire. To tell ye more would be needless, for ye would no more understand the truth of the Gate than a man of my village would have understood the power that drives a musket ball on its errand of death. He would have thought it magic, but he could have fired a musket, once shown the method. So it is with ye and the mysteries of the Gate. Remember then my instructions and take care that . . ."

I never found out what Pew wanted me to take care of. At that moment, he fell very noisily asleep. In a second he was doing his buzz saw imitation again.

I looked over at Matty and said, "You ready?"

"As I'll ever be, I guess," he replied.

So there in the moonlight, we went through the procedure Abner Pew had shown us a month before. We faced his stone, did the turn and walked into February, 1942.

5

How Do You Do, '42?

It took us about an hour in the past to realize we knew next to nothing about the year 1942. All the study and memory drill with Matty wasn't exactly wasted, but close to it. I got the first clue when we hitchhiked into New York City.

There was very little traffic on the road when we walked out of the cemetery entrance. I figured it was because of gas rationing. I later found out it was for a much different reason. In 1942, Branford wasn't the commuter town it is today. It was just a small town, way out in the boonies. The reason for no traffic was simple. There just wasn't any cause for a person to be in Branford after eleven o'clock at night. We must have waited for a half hour before we even saw a car come down the road headed for New York. First we saw the lights, then the car. I was in position real fast, with my thumb in the air, when Matty grabbed my arm.

"Richie, look!" he gasped. "It's a Chrysler Airflow!"

I guessed Matty was right. He always is when it comes to old cars. The Airflow pulled up on the side of the road, and I got a better look at it. It was a four-door sedan, shaped like no car made before or since. If you've ever seen those old drawings where an artist years ago showed what the future would look like, you've seen cars like the Airflow. They were like huge Volkswagen beetles, but with a much flatter rear and front grille. It was really a kick to see one rolling down a highway, instead of behind a velvet rope at an auto show. This one was waiting for us, so we hurried up and got to it.

This middle-aged guy was driving. He looked us over pretty good before he unlocked the door. I guess we must have looked harmless enough. I got in front, and Matty piled into the back. The driver started up, and as we drove toward New York, he said, "Kinda late to be out thumbing, isn't it, fellows?" He gave us another hard look. I was beginning to wonder what it was all about. "Do you two live around here?" he asked.

"Sure do, sir," said Matty from the back. "We're going into town to catch Glenn Miller at the Paramount tomorrow morning."

"Oh," said the driver, nodding his head. "That explains it. Can't be too careful, y'know. They spotted that German submarine off the Narrows last week. The police think they may have been dropping off spies or saboteurs."

I knew then what he was talking about. When the war first broke out, there were a lot of spy scares. A lot of people thought it was hysteria. "War nerves" they called it. But it turned out later that there really were submarines landing spies in the New York area. The Narrows that the driver was talking about is the Atlantic Ocean entrance to New York harbor.

"Gosh," said Matty in his con man's tone. "You didn't think we were spies, did you?"

"Not after you told me who was playing at the Paramount, I didn't," answered the driver. "I didn't think the Nazis had any colored spies, either, but I didn't want to take any chances."

I made a mental note. The driver had said "colored," meaning black, when he referred to Matty. All I'd read in my books led me to believe that the word was "Negro" in 1942. I got another surprise when I asked the driver, "You're pretty lucky to have gasoline for this drive, aren't you?"

I was talking about gas rationing. I looked in the corner of his windshield, but I didn't see any sticker. Either it was too dark inside the car to see, or he didn't have one. I was just about to comment on it when I got a nudge from Matty in the back seat. But the driver was answering my question.

"I sure am. I don't think there's a gas station open between here and Flushing at this hour. But I filled up in Garden City before I left. No trouble. You can't hoard gas. No place to put it. I guess it'll be different if they put through this gas rationing thing they're talking about on the radio.".

I exhaled silently. I'd nearly made a bad mistake. Rationing for gas hadn't come in yet. In the meantime, Matty was still prodding me from in back. I turned to look over my shoulder, but Matty gave me the face-front-don't-look-back glance. I was wondering what the heck was going on.

"Speaking of radio," said the driver, "it's eleven-thirty. They got the news on WNEW now."

He reached over to the dashboard and turned a knob. For a while, nothing happened. That, at least, I was ready for. In 1942, they didn't have any transistors, just radio tubes. They have to warm up before the radio will play. There was a buzzing and some crackly static, then a voice faded in, ". . . *in a retreat up the Bataan Peninsula. Meanwhile, Japanese Imperial troops have completely devastated the open city of Manila with artillery and air attacks. This is in complete disregard of the Geneva Convention for open cities. Reports of atrocities committed on helpless civilians continue to pour in. Our armies in the Philippines, under General Douglas MacArthur, are returning enemy fire and inflicting heavy casualties.*"

"Dirty, sneaky bastards," said the driver. "I hope they kill 'em all."

Matty gave me another nudge and began to hum a tune. It was *On Top Of Old Smokey*. I thought for a minute he'd lost his marbles. The radio broadcast continued: "*On the home front, two Queens men were arrested yesterday for price gouging on items for which there is strategic need—automobile tires, coffee, and sugar. . . .*"

"How about that?" snorted the driver. "Here we are in a war, and those bums can only think of making money off it. They oughta be shot!"

Matty was giving me the nudge again. I had already figured out that he wanted to tell me something the driver shouldn't hear. But what? I took a stab. "Thinking about the show at the Paramount tomorrow, Matty?" I asked.

"No," Matty answered, "I was just thinking what a swell car this is."

The driver picked it up like a cue. "You're right," he said. "A lotta people think they're ugly, but I got this car brand new in 1936. She's got 40,000 miles on her, and she runs like a top. Gets eighteen miles to the gallon, too."

"Reminds me of somebody in Branford with one. He's crazy about it, also."

My mind was spinning. What was Matty running on about? I know there isn't a Chrysler Airflow anywhere in

Branford. I was worried, too. If Matty made some kind of slip about the future, or even the "now" of 1942, we could be in bad trouble. The whole city, it seemed, was up in the air about spies. But there wasn't any way I could get Matty's attention off it. I sat there in horror as he went on.

"Great cars. Four-wheel hydraulic brakes, safety glass all around, big engine . . ."

"Oh, I ain't got the big engine," said the driver. "I got the six cylinder."

"Really?" said Matty. "I didn't know that there was a Chrysler six."

"There ain't," said the driver. "This here's a De Soto. What'd you think, it was the Chrysler?"

"Yeah."

"Lotta people make that mistake. They look a lot alike. But this here's a De Soto. I thought I knew everyone in this part of the island with an Airflow car, though. What's your friend's name?"

My heart sank. I not only didn't know what Matty was getting at, but this guy obviously knew the area real well. If Matty put his foot in it, we could find ourselves in jail pretty quick!

"I don't know his real name," said Matty. "The guys in town call him by his nickname." At this point, Matty nudged me again.

"What's the nickname?" asked the driver.

"Smokey Bear," said Matty.

It came on me like a sunrise. I turned full around and looked into the back seat. Sure enough, there was a uniform of some sort on a hanger near the back door of the car. Blessedly, Matty hadn't tipped the driver off with his "Smokey Bear" line. That was CB slang that wouldn't be understood for thirty years yet. The driver never tumbled.

"Smokey Behr?" he asked. "Sounds German. Or does he spell it like Max Baer, the fighter?"

"Like the fighter," I answered. I was safe there. I knew that Max Baer had been heavyweight champion of the world in the '30's. And he was Jewish. No Nazis there, at least.

"Well, tell him next time you see him, there's a guy named George Binns in Garden City has a De Soto and would like to talk sometime, willya?"

"George Binns," I said, like I was sure to tell old Smokey. "How can he reach you?"

"Oh, I'm in the Garden City phone book. Or he could even reach me on my job. I'm a special police officer at Macy's department store in town. Just have him call the main number for Macy's, ask for security, then for me. I'm there five nights, from twelve to eight in the morning."

I breathed a little easier. The guy was only a rent-a-cop. I had visions of both me and Matty in the pokey for a while there.

"Sure thing, Mr. Binns," I said. "I'll tell Smokey next time I see him."

The radio newscast ended, and George Binns snapped it off. We rode in silence for a few, then Binns spoke up again. "You boys gonna wait for the draft, or are you gonna enlist right away?"

I knew the proper answer to that one. Everyone in the country was volunteering in 1942. It showed you were a real patriot, not waiting to be drafted.

"We're too young to be drafted," I said to George Binns. "But next month, when we turn eighteen, we're going to join the Marines."

"Good lads!" said George. "I tried, but they don't want me. I'm over forty, and I got two kids. I missed the war with Kaiser, too. You got all the luck, you kids."

"Yeah," I said, "we'll be out there fighting the Nazis in no time."

"Get one or two for me," said George Binns, savagely.

We spent the rest of the ride into New York saying as little as possible. I could see right from the start, this had to be the way. Matty and I had done a lot of studying, but it was like studying for a history exam. We had no real idea what people in the '40's talked about on a day-to-day basis. If that wasn't enough, we'd almost made some bad mistakes with George Binns. So clearly the thing to do was shut up and listen to what others said.

George Binns dropped us off just the other side of the 59th Street Bridge into Manhattan. It was a clear, chilly night. We were glad for the old-style overcoats and suits we'd bought from thrift shops. They might have looked baggy and turkey, but they were sure warm. I was a little worried about our shoes. They weren't 1940's. I couldn't get any. But men's shoes haven't changed too much over the years. The ones we wore were low-top, with laces. Near as I could see from people passing by, we fitted right in.

It was after midnight, but the city was still busy. If I'd expected the whole town to be blacked out as an air raid precaution, I was sure wrong. The city was lit up like there was no such thing as a war.

We started walking west. I knew that all the great jazz clubs were on or around West 52nd Street. We were at East 59th and Second Avenue. When we reached Third Avenue, there it was. The Third Avenue El! I'd read about it and seen pictures of it. Just as we walked under the huge steel overhead structure, a train passed overhead. Talk about a racket! It made me wonder how people could live in the buildings on either side of the street. And as if the El trains weren't enough, they had trolley cars running underneath the El. Matty and I were standing under the 59th Street station when we saw the trolley coming down Third Avenue. I'd never seen or been on a trolley car in my life. Matty and I exchanged glances.

"You up for it?" I asked.

"Do we know where this one is going?" countered Matty. I glanced at the front of the red and cream-colored streetcar as it approached us.

"It says CROSSTOWN on the front," I said, "but it's headed downtown, now. It must turn west somewhere along the line. C'mon. Let's try it!"

The conductor of the trolley spotted us in the pickup area and brought the big noisy streetcar to a stop. The doors opened, and a few folks got off. We stepped on. The motorman (I found out later that's what they were called, not conductors) took my silver dollar without a second glance and gave me a buck's worth of change. I put two nickels into the fare box and off we went.

It was a kicky ride. The trolley stopped smack in the middle of Times Square, and we got off. It was right out of a history book or an old movie on late-night TV. The New York Times building had an illuminated strip that ran all around it. The news of the day was spelled out in lights and ran around the building on the strip. As we watched, the lights spelled out GERMAN SIEGE OF LENINGRAD CONTINUES . . . NAZI ARMY WITHIN FIVE MILES OF CITY . . . RUSSIAN ARMY STILL HOLDING OUT . . .

But Times Square was something else. If you've ever been there, the only thing you would have recognized was the sign for Camel cigarettes, with the guy on it blowing smoke rings. It's done with a steam line, and it looks like the guy painted on the billboard is doing it. That sign is still there today. But all the rest was different. The Paramount and the Astor theaters (long gone now) were there. But at the moment, all we had eyes for was the marquee on the Paramount. It read,

JOEL MC CREA   VERONICA LAKE
IN
PRESTON STURGES'
"SULLIVAN'S TRAVELS"
ONSTAGE
THE GLENN MILLER ORCHESTRA

We discovered that we'd missed the last stage show at
the Paramount, so we walked around the Times Square
area, taking it all in. I don't know how Matty felt those
first few hours; I never did ask him. But me, I felt like I'd
come home. The whole atmosphere felt comfortable to
me. Sure, things were strange, but not all that different
from 1976. And certain things were still there. Like the
N.Y. Times tower and most of the older buildings. I
think the biggest shocker was West 52nd Street when
we got there. Today, the street between Seventh and
Sixth Avenues is almost all office-type, high-rise buildings. But then! It was row and row of three- and four-
story buildings, and it seemed each one housed a night-
club featuring Jazz. We were like a couple of kids in
a candy store. Walking up and down, grabbing each
other's arm and pointing out who was playing at each
club.

I'll give you an idea: At Roseland Ballroom, Stan Kenton
and his Orchestra were wailing. The Famous Door had
Red Allen, with J.C. Higgenbotham on trombone, but
we had just missed seeing another great. There was a
sign still up reading THE BENNY CARTER BAND, featuring
Dizzy Gillespie on trumpet! And in between each building, any place a poster could be glued up, was the ad for
the Apollo Theater up in Harlem. The star of their stage
show was Louis Armstrong!

Trouble with our first night in town was that we got in
too late. We heard Red Allen at the Famous Door, and
he was so great we spent almost the whole night in that

little, dingy place. I don't think it could have held more than sixty people. By the time we got out, we'd missed the rest of the "street," as the musicians called it back then. But when we got to the far west end of 52nd Street, we could have kicked ourselves.

The place was Kelly's Stable, at 137 West 52nd. The sign outside read:

THE SABBY LEWIS ORCHESTRA

PLUS

THE KING COLE TRIO

If you're not a big jazz fan, you wouldn't know about the Sabby Lewis Band. Like I said, there were some really great bands back then that didn't make any recordings, or long tours. The Sabby Lewis Band was out of Boston, and, in addition to being a great band, was one of the few orchestras that had black and white guys playing together. They only made two or three records, and on some off-the-wall label called Crystaltone. Today, those records are worth a lot of money.

But I guess what really knocked us out was the chance to see the King Cole Trio. Back then, that's what Nat Cole called himself. Not many people today realize that Nat Cole was one of the best jazz pianists in the country before he started singing those creamy-dreamy ballads. And his bass player, Wesley Prince, and his guitarist, Oscar Moore, were two of the toughest dudes on the set. And we'd missed them!

We promised ourselves that tomorrow, Saturday, after we'd caught Glenn Miller at the Paramount, and the afternoon show at the Apollo with Louis Armstrong, we'd come back and catch Nat Cole and the Sabby Lewis Band. We were both tired and ready to call it a night. We went back to the Broadway area to look for a hotel that wouldn't cost too much. We'd already spent fifteen dollars from my stash of sixty-five silver dollars, and money might be a problem soon.

We couldn't get a hotel that would take both Matty and me. It took a while for it to sink in on us. Most of the nicer cheap hotels told us they were full up. When we got to a smaller one on 48th Street, west of Eighth Avenue, the desk clerk wasn't that nice. He took one look at us and said, "Why don't you try the YMCA on Central Park West? We don't take colored here."

I grabbed Matty before he could say anything and whispered to him, "Cool it, babe. We can't make a fuss. If this crumb calls the cops, we don't have any I.D. The way George Binns was scared of spies, we could have more grief than this is worth."

Matty didn't say a word. He nodded, and we walked out of the lobby. We were so tired that instead of taking the subway or a trolley uptown, we hailed a cab. The driver knew where the Y was, and within the half hour we were in a room at the YMCA. I knew Matty was upset. He hadn't said a word since we'd left the lobby of that fleabag hotel. I was ready to go to my own room. I said good-night and started for the door. Matty stopped me.

"Richie?"

"Yeah, Matt?"

"Tomorrow, after we see the groups we came to see, I want out. I don't think I can hack this."

"Aw, come on, Matty," I said. "Just because of that creep at the hotel?"

"No, not just him. It's the whole country, you know. This is 1942, man. I think the only places we could go together in the whole city, we've been to tonight. Face it, the color line don't mean diddly to musicians. It never really has. But no way I'm gonna spend my life shuffling and saying 'Yassuh Boss' . . . No way in the world. After tomorrow night, Richie, I want to start looking for the Future Gate and get back home."

I felt in my overcoat pocket for the big iron key I'd gotten from Abner Pew. I tried to remember what he'd said about how to locate the Future Gate. It had been something about the horizon and the sea and the key glowing and getting warm when you were close. To tell the truth, the reason I hadn't paid too much attention was that I wasn't really interested in going back. What was there for me in 1976? My mom? Harry? Forget it.

But Matty was a different thing. I guess I'd been so carried away with escaping to the Past that I forgot it wouldn't be so great in this country for a black man in 1942. It ain't all that swift in 1976, but I just didn't know how really bad it was in 1942. How could I? There are some things that they don't mention in history books. But then again, most history books are written by whites.

I looked over at Matty. He was lying on the bed, looking at the ceiling. He was really down. I didn't know what I was talking about, but I said, "Sure thing. Tomorrow night, after Nat Cole and Sabby Lewis, we look for the Gate to the Future."

"Yeah," grunted Matty. "Where do you think we're gonna start?"

"I'm not sure," I admitted, "but Pew gave us the signs. Anyway, I'm whipped. Can we plan it tomorrow?"

"Sure, man," said Matty in a flat voice.

I went to my room after saying good-night and did some staring at the ceiling myself. It had all seemed like such a great idea. Now it was turning sour. And the fact was, I had no more idea where to start looking than Matty did. I did my best to recall exactly what Abner Pew had said about the Gate location. He'd said, "Where the compass needle spins, and the horizon changes places with the sea . . ."

I had the nagging idea in the back of my mind that I'd heard something very much like that. And not from Abner Pew, either. But try as I might, I couldn't recall. I fell asleep still trying.

6

Love, Your Magic Spell
Is Everywhere

We got another surprise the next morning when we subwayed down to Times Square to the Paramount. The line! We had intended to take in the first show of the day. That's because the admission before noon was, if you're ready, a big fifty cents. That's for a first-run flick, and the Glenn Miller Band live. But we weren't the only ones who had the same idea. The line started up near the box office and went around the corner and halfway down the block. And the box office wasn't even open yet! We looked at it, and Matty said, "What do you think, man? Is it worth the line?"

"We got few things more than time, Matty," I pointed out. "Besides, this theater is huge. I don't think it'll even be crowded once we're all inside."

We walked around the block and got on the end of the line. It was mostly young people like ourselves. Right in front of us were two chicks, one a swift-looking redhead and the other a dynamite black chick. Evidently they were together. They kept looking around and talking and laughing together. I had a quick conference with Matty.

"You want to have a try with them?"

"I dunno," said Matty. "After last night, I just don't care too much . . ."

"Aw, c'mon, babe," I said. "There's a big difference between some clown at a hotel desk and a couple of chicks our age. You know pretty well it's even different in 1976 with older people."

Matty looked ahead on the line to the two girls. "They ain't that hard to take," he admitted, "but I'm telling you, the first chill we get from them, I bug off. No fooling, Rich."

"Gotcha," I replied, and tried to figure out an opening line. The best I could come up with was to the black chick, who was right in front of me. She was wearing a tan raincoat and so help me, it had writing all over it. I don't mean like a print thing. The raincoat had started out plain. All the writing obviously had been done by hand. It had autographs from friends, and here and there a single word or phrase, like "Solid" and in another spot, "Cookin' with gas!" Most of the autographs said "To Sheila." Besides the raincoat, she was wearing a red sweater, verrry tight, a medium-length plaid skirt, and so help me, brown and white saddle shoes with ankle socks over nylons. Except I guess they weren't nylons. Nylon wasn't invented yet. That I knew. I took a stab at conversation with her.

"Say, that's a swell coat, Sheila."

I knew it was a lame line soon as I said it. But that's the way it always is with me. On the way home, I think of all the great shouldasaids. I was also being careful about the way I said things. I could make a slip and talk in 1976, and either get frosted or maybe even arrested.

I guess the line wasn't as turkey as I thought. The black chick gave me a smile and said, "How'd you know my name was Sheila?"

That's when Matty surprised me and stepped in. Now this is a dude who's never lost for words.

"Had to be," he said. "We didn't think your name was Solid or even Cookin'. All that leaves is To My Best Friend or Love or maybe Sheila. We just hadda guess at Sheila."

The black girl looked Matty over like he was some new kind of animal.

"You two friends?" she asked.

"The best of," said Matty.

The black girl turned to her friend, the redhead. They whispered together for a few seconds. Once in a while, they'd look over at us and giggle, then go back to what they were saying. Wow. I haven't heard a girl giggle since I was in kindergarten. Sheila finished her conversation with the redhead and turned to us.

"This is my girl friend, Lorraine, fellas," she said. The redhead gave us a nice, friendly smile.

Matty took over. "Delighted, ladies," he said. "This swift dude here is my main man, Richie. I'm Matty."

The girls looked at Matty like he had flowers growing out of his head. I knew right away what had happened. Matty had gone into his suave, Joe Cool routine for picking up chicks. Trouble was, he was talking pure 1976.

Lorraine actually burst out laughing. Matty wasn't amused, but who would be? He was coming on as usual, in a way that's always worked before. But he was getting laughs. Lorraine picked up on his expression.

"Sorry, Matty," she said, swallowing still another laugh, "but you talk so funny. Where are you two fellas from?" It was the first time she'd said anything, and it took me by surprise. She had a Brooklynese accent you couldn't have dented with a sledgehammer. Matty and I both answered her.

"Long Island," said Matty.

"Branford," I said at the same time. It came out jumbled up, and it was good for some more giggles from the chicks. But it broke the ice. In a few minutes, we were rapping back and forth like old friends.

"You fellas gonna sit in the balcony?" asked Lorraine.

"Hadn't thought about it one way or another," I said. "What's the difference?"

"Boy, you two sure are strange guys," said Sheila, giving us a hard look.

"You can smoke in the balcony. Unless, of course, you don't smoke . . ."

I could tell from the way she said it, that smoking was the "in" thing for people my age in 1942. Neither Matty nor I smoke. Cigarettes, that is. I used to, back when I thought it was hip and made me look older. Then they showed us that cancer flick in school, and I changed my mind about how hip it is to die of lung rot. Sheila had reached into her raincoat pocket and produced a pack of Lucky Strikes. It took me a while to realize what they were. The pack was dark, dark green, with a red and gold bulls-eye. I never saw anything like it. But I wanted to come off as the cool one for a change. I took the cigarette she offered. Matty passed. I think cigarettes must be made milder nowadays. This one nearly burned out my throat. I wasn't turkey enough to cough, but tears came to my eyes.

"Say, Richie," said Sheila, "you don't really smoke, do you?"

"I did," I said, "but I gave it up. My doctor says it's bad for you."

"You believe that junk?" said Sheila. "Look at the magazines. Bing Crosby, Ty Power, they all smoke. If it was that bad, would they do it?"

I wasn't about to go into the Surgeon General's report, for obvious reasons, so I only said, "They're just not for me. I have asthma attacks, sometimes."

Sheila gave me the sweetest smile. She reached over and put her hand on my shoulder. It was the first time, outside of crowds, that I'd actually been physically touched by someone from 1942. It didn't make me mad, I might add.

"You mean you took a cigarette, even though you didn't want it?" she asked. "Why should you do a thing like that?"

"Well, I didn't want you to think I was, er . . . a . . ." I searched my mind in wild desperation. The word I wanted to say was either "turkey" or "square." I couldn't for the life of me recall what the 1942 word was, if I ever knew.

Sheila came to my rescue. "A drip or a square from Delaware?" she asked. "That's all right, Richie. I think you're all right. Even if you are a little strange, you're a nice boy."

"Yeah," added Lorraine in Brooklynese. "We seen some strange boids on this line. Youse two are all right." But she was looking at Matty when she said it.

I don't know why it jarred me so to hear a girl as pretty as Lorraine talk in a killer accent like that. It kinda spoiled the picture, if you get what I mean. In 1976, you hardly hear anyone with a real heavy accent of any kind, anymore. I read somewhere that it's TV and radio that have done it. All the TV people and D.J.'s talk in pretty much the same way. Nowadays, if anybody talks in Brooklynese on the tube, it's a comedy character. But Lorraine was no comedy character. She was very real, very pretty and as near as I could see, very interested in Matty. And Sheila seemed to dig me.

I'll tell you, it was some turnaround from the night before, when we couldn't even get a place to sleep for money. I was wrapped up in what I was thinking and didn't realize that Sheila had asked me a question. She was looking at me, obviously expecting an answer.

"Sorry, Sheila," I said. "I was thinking of something. What did you say?"

"I said will you two guys go and save our seats when the doors open?" She pointed to the long line ahead of us. "Last week, we almost got trampled trying to get decent seats in the balcony."

Matty picked up on her cue right away. "No sweat, sister," he smiled. "We'll get you the best. Where do you want to sit in the balcony? We'll meet you there. You can't miss us, we'll be laying down on four seats."

"Foist balcony, foist row," said Lorraine. "And Matty . . ."

"Yeah?"

"When yez go in, don't take the big center stairs up to the balcony. Go in like for the orchestra section and take a side stair. They ain't gonna be jammed up like the main stairs."

"Gotcha," said Matty. "Can we buy your tickets, girls?"

"Jeez, that'd be swell, Matty," said Lorraine with a smile that lit up Times Square. "Hey, look. The line's moving. The doors must be open!"

She was right. So was I. As big as the line was, it moved very quickly. No doubt about it, the Paramount was some big theater. We got up to the box office and got the tickets. The line was very orderly until it passed the ticket-taker's line into the huge, ornate lobby. Then all hell broke loose. All the kids our age were running around like crazy, trying to get up the stairway in the center of the lobby. Matty and I flat out ran to a side stair and found it only medium crowded. It took some doing, but we got four seats together in the second row of the center aisle of the first balcony. The first row was already full up. The girls hadn't shown yet, so Matty and I had time for a council of war before they arrived.

"How do you want them to sit when they get here?" he asked me.

"What do you mean?"

"Come on, turkey. Which chick do you want? I think the sister has eyes for you."

"You come on," I replied. "This ain't any 1976, man. Outside of us, these girls are the only salt-and-pepper team I've seen in 1942. You seem to have gotten over last night pretty quick."

Matty let out a big laugh. "You are forgetting, bro, that it's dark in here once the show goes on. What's that they say about in the dark . . . ?"

"Maybe so," I said, "but I think the hip thing to do is leave the two seats between us empty. That way, they can sit where they want, OK?"

"You're on," said Matty. "But I'm telling you that Lorraine is gonna sit next to me, and Sheila is gonna glom onto you like a shot."

"No way."

"I got five says she does," smiled Matty.

Just then, the girls showed up. Without word one, they moved into the aisle and sat exactly like Matty said they would. I couldn't miss the look he gave me.

"Candy?" asked Sheila, holding out a bag. "Since you guys paid for us, we got a lot at the stand downstairs."

I looked at the assortment of stuff in the bag. I guess even candy has changed over the years. The only thing I recognized was a Clark bar. The rest of it had funny names I never heard of. No popcorn, either. I asked about it. Sheila laughed.

"Where do you think you are, some neighborhood itch? This is the Paramount, honey. They don't have trash like that here. And all the nickel candy costs a dime, too."

I had to laugh, inside. I wonder what Sheila would think of the price of candy bars in 1976? But what didn't make me laugh was that when Sheila said it, she reached over and put her hand on mine. I wasn't mad, you understand. Far from it. Just surprised. Then the lights dimmed and the whole crowd in the balcony began to applaud. The curtains on the huge stage began to part. At the same time, a curtain behind the big curtains went straight up. The first item was a newsreel.

I've since found out that the last newsreel made was in 1967. I'd seen pieces of newsreels shown on TV, but never a whole one. It was something else. It was called Movietone News. I was so into the newsreel, I was surprised to get a little nudge from Sheila sitting next to me.

"Sorry, Sheila," I said. "I was watching the show. Did you say something?"

"Honey, it's only the newsreel," she smiled. "Nobody watches the newsreel. Even Matty. Look."

I glanced across to Matty and Lorraine. In the darkness, I could still see that Matty's arm was draped across the back of the movie seat and Lorraine's shoulder. And they were holding hands, too. I wondered just how cool Matty was being. I also wondered what I was going to do. I'd never been out with a black chick even in 1976. When Matty and I had double-dated, we'd gone either with two white chicks or if Matty had had a black date, one white, one black. Come right down to it, I didn't really know any black girls except for Matty's sisters. I needn't have worried. When I put my arm over the seatback, Sheila snuggled close and rested her head on my shoulder. By the time the newsreel ended and the main feature began, you could say we were more than friendly.

I can't tell you too much about *Sullivan's Travels*, the movie we saw. I was much more interested in Sheila. I do remember that it was about this dude, Joel McCrea, who wanted to go out to see how poor folks lived or some such crap. But I won't forget the scene where McCrea and Veronica Lake kissed for the first time. I mean, there they were, two giant heads on the movie screen, their lips plastered together. It seemed so natural that Sheila and I did, too. The rest of the movie drifted by after that. I don't recall how it ended. I was busy.

There was a short break between the movie and the stage show. The houselights came on again. Both Sheila and Lorraine knew the drill. They told us how long the break would be and excused themselves for the ladies' room. Matty and I talked while they were gone.

"Hey, Richie," Matty laughed, "you got a kleenex with you?"

"What for?" I asked.

"Because folks has lied to y'awl," he replied in a phony down-home accent. "It seems it do rub off. Wipe your face, man. It's full of lipstick."

I passed my hand over my mouth. It felt a little slick. When I looked at my hand, it was smeared with a bright red. Nineteen forty-two girls were big on lipstick. And it seemed the brighter the red color, the better. I reached into my back pocket and took out a handkerchief. I'd taken some because I wasn't sure if kleenex was being used in 1942. I gave one to Matty, too. He wiped his mouth and said, "Too bad these chicks don't wear black lipstick, like in the flick. It wouldn't show on me that way."

He was kidding, of course. Lipstick in old flicks photographed as black. It was really red, though. And if it comes to that, Matty isn't a very dark-skinned black man, either. You could see the lipstick as plain on him as on me.

The girls came back to their seats just as the house-lights began to dim again.

"Sorry," said Sheila to me. "What a crowd in the ladies' room!"

"Sure you weren't talking about Matty and me?" I asked.

Sheila smiled. "That, too," she said. Just then, the lights on the stage came up, the curtains parted, and there they were, playing *Moonlight Serenade*. The one and only original Glenn Miller Band!

It was dynamite. I can't tell you. There's all the difference in the world between those scratchy 78 RPM records or even the non-stereo reissues of that band. When they swung into *String of Pearls*, the sound could have lifted you out of your chair! Forget rock concerts, man. Oh, they're loud. But that's amplifier and electronic loud. This was an honest-to-God, unelectrified band, and they were smoking! Down on the orchestra floor, kids were getting up and dancing in the aisles. The place was a mad house. Ushers were trying to get the kids to sit down, but forget it. The kids in the balcony were getting up to dance now. Sheila got to her feet.

"C'mon Richie," she said, "let's cut a rug!"

Now, I dig dancing. I'm not much at it, though. Few musicians are. I guess we spend so much time on the bandstand making the sounds, we don't get much chance to dance. I watched the steps the kids around us were doing in the semi-darkness.

"I don't know, Sheila . . ." I began.

"Aw, Richie," she said sadly. "Can't you lindy?"

I looked over at the kids dancing again. Looked to me like this lindy dance she was talking about wasn't too different from some varieties of the hustle I've seen done.

"Sure!" I said, getting to my feet. "Let's do it!"

I shouldn't have been concerned. It was so jammed in the aisle, we didn't have room to do much of anything. In fact, I don't think I've been that close to so many strangers in my life. We had to give up and go back to our seats. Before you knew it, the show was over, and the houselights came on

Sheila was glowing; Matty and Lorraine were tighter than ticks on a dog. Lorraine leaned over and hollered above the noise of the audience moving out, "Jeez, it was great! You gonna stay for the next show?"

I couldn't believe it. "You mean you want to see the whole show over again?" I asked.

"Sure! Whaddayou think, we're gonna go home now? We just hang around for a little until it starts again. One show for a half a buck? We ain't Rockefeller, y'know."

That knocked me out. A big half a buck! But then again, if the prices were any indication, salaries were probably lower, too.

"You girls forgetting we picked up the tickets?" asked Matty. "There's other places we could go to."

Lorraine and Sheila exchanged glances. I got the feeling that they wanted to talk it over. I said so, and they had a mini-conference. While they were talking, I got together with Matty.

"Listen, man," I said, "you've gotta cool it. You already made so many mistakes talking out of 1976 to these chicks, we've been just lucky nothing got picked up on. And besides, where can we take them? A mixed couple in a restaurant ain't anything in New York in 1976. But 1942 is something else, again."

Matty only smiled. "You're forgetting that there's two couples. Who's gonna know who's with who? You look at us and most people assume me and Sheila are together, anyway."

"I guess you're right. But where can we go? I don't want to run into any static. We can't afford it," I said.

"Hey, dummy, we're going to the Apollo from here, aren't we?"

"Yeah. Are you forgetting the grief we had from those black dudes at that concert?"

"Don't sweat it," said Matty. "In 1942, they still liked having whitey come uptown. It'll be cool, you'll see."

The girls came back from their rap, and I could tell from the look on Sheila's face that the news wasn't good. She came up to me and said, "Richie, I'm sorry. I don't think we could go anywhere."

"Was it something we did or said?" I asked.

"No, hon. You did and said just fine. It's the race thing that's got us worried. I mean, it's different with Lorraine and me. We're in the same class in school, and we've been going to places together a long time. But with fellas, it's different." She took my hand. "You're a real sweet guy, Richie. But I don't think you know what you'd be letting yourself in for. Lorraine and me, we get trouble even in our high school just because we're good friends . . ."

I was so relieved, I laughed out loud. Sheila didn't know why, and she looked let out.

"Sheila, honey," I said, "don't give it another thought. Matty and I were talking about the exact same thing. We were afraid that you didn't know the troubles we could have. Not to worry. We were going up to the Apollo to hear Louis Armstrong. Would you like to come? On us?"

She gave me that smile again, kind of like the sun coming out, and nodded yes. We left the balcony of the Paramount walking on air. But we were cool enough to change partners when we hit the street.

As we headed for the uptown IRT subway that would take us to Harlem, I said to Matty, "What do you think of February 7th, 1942?"

Matty gave me a huge wink and said, "I think things are pickin' up, man."

We got the subway and headed uptown.

7

Jumpin' at the Apollo

If I thought I had seen a band break up a theater when the Miller group made the Paramount swing, I was wrong. Because when Louis and the band came onstage at the Apollo, babe, that was it. That band could have blown a hole straight through a piece of iron. What a sound! Louis never sounded better. I was a little let out to discover that Jack Teagarden wasn't playing trombone with Louis back then. Turned out he was still playing in the Midwest.

But the dude he did have on first-chair trombone was no slouch, let me tell you. He looked a lot like Louis. Satchmo even made jokes about that on stage. The 'bone man's name was, no kidding, George Washington. When Louis announced his name, Matty leaned over to me and whispered, "He sure don't blow like the father of our country!"

"You're right," I said. "He blows more like a mother!"

We drew blank gazes from Lorraine and Sheila when

we both broke up. But I guess they were getting used to us saying strange things. I'd made a few slipups on the subway heading uptown, nothing far out, but enough to make Sheila ask me, "Richie, are you and Matty for sure from Long Island?"

"Sure are, hon. Just over near Garden City, if you know where that is."

"I heard the name, but I've never been there," she said. "In fact, I never been much of anywhere but Brooklyn and Times Square once a week. Do you know, I've never been to the Apollo?"

"That's OK, hon. I never have, either. It didn't seem cool enough to go there."

Sheila gave me another blank look. "They got air conditioning. I see it on their signs. Besides, this is February. What do you care how cool it is?"

"Yeah, you're right," I said lamely. After all, how could I explain "cool"?

And as usual, Matty was right. As mixed couples, we didn't draw any more than a casual glance on West 125th Street, walking to the Apollo. I was really impressed by 125th Street in 1942. The only way you see it today, if you're white, is in newscasts, and it looks grim. But back then, it was . . . well, elegant is the word. The stores were all first-rate; there weren't any buildings that looked bombed out. And being Saturday afternoon, it seemed everyone in Harlem was out either shopping, window-shopping or just plain strolling around.

Feeling pretty cool, excuse the expression, we went into the Apollo. We'd timed it right, and there wasn't a line outside.

There was a whole stage show along with the Louis Armstrong Band. Dancers, singers and all. I only remember a big, heavy lady who sang the blues. Her name was Louise Beavers. As to the rest, Sheila and I had eyes·

only for each other. But when Louis was playing, look out!

By the time we'd left the Apollo, it was already getting dark, and the day was turning chilly. I was hungry, and the girls said they could stand a bite. We had some of the best ribs, rice with brown gravy, and cornbread I ever tasted at a place on West 127th Street off Lenox Avenue. The place was called Tiny's. There really was a Tiny, too. He was the host and about the size of a fat Abner Pew, if you can conceive of any one man being that size. Not only were we given the best of food, we got the best of service and treatment from Tiny, himself.

We paid the check at Tiny's. It came to a big four dollars with tip. I walked out onto the street with Sheila's hand in mine, feeling better about being in 1942 in Harlem than I ever felt anywhere in 1976. It was a real bring-down when the girls said they had to go home. I had figured we had dates for the rest of the night. But as Lorraine explained, "We'd love to, fellas, but we gotta be home by ten, or our folks will really give it to us. Sheila's dad is tougher than mine. And we gotta go all the way to Jefferson Street and Howard Avenue in Brooklyn."

"What part of Brooklyn is that?" I asked. See, I thought if it wasn't too far, Matty and I could take the girls home, then still come back and catch Nat Cole and the Sabby Lewis Band later on.

"That's the Bedford-Stuyvesant section," Lorraine answered. I nearly dropped my teeth. Then I realized that in 1942, Bedford-Stuyvesant was a real nice neighborhood, not the ghetto it is today.

"It's all right, Richie," said Sheila. "I know Brooklyn is way out of your way. We can go alone. We do it every Saturday after the matinee at the Paramount."

"But when and how will I see you again?" I asked, not

realizing how important it was to me until I'd said the words. They must have been the right words.

Sheila gave my arm a little squeeze and said, "We'll be on line at the Paramount next Saturday."

"That's not what I mean," I said. "I mean, what's your address? Your telephone number?"

"We don't have phones," put in Lorraine, "but if you call HE 3–5694—that's the candy store downstairs in our building—they'll call us to the phone."

"Or if you want," said Sheila, "you can tell me when you're gonna call, and I can be there." She smiled. "I wouldn't mind waiting for your call."

Man, what a difference from chicks in 1976. What with all the women's lib, I don't think there's a chick alive in 1976 who'd admit that she'd hang around a place just waiting for some dude to call her. No doubt about it, I was digging 1942 more and more.

"You won't have to wait," I said, surprising myself again. "I'll call you tomorrow at noon."

"Uh, could you make that at two o'clock, Richie?" she asked.

"Sure thing. Why?"

"Well, tomorrow's Sunday, and I sing in the church choir. I won't be back until after one o'clock."

"Wow!" I said. "You mean, you sing gospel music? I can't believe it. After jazz and blues, gospel is some of my favorite music in the world!"

"I never knew a white boy like you, Richie," she said. "Lorraine is my best friend, and she doesn't know anything about sanctified music. I mean, she goes to her church; I go to mine. You sure are some strange white boy, Richie."

"You know many white guys?" I asked, hating myself for asking. I didn't want to know. I didn't care. But I did.

She gave me a shy look and said, "No, Richie. You're

the first white boy I ever went out with. I just meant all the boys I meet in school, that's all."

I felt like a fool. This black chick with the beautiful smile had me all turned around. If I had to admit it, I guess the word was jealous. And I knew it was silly. Why should I be jealous with a girl I'd only known for a few hours? But I was.

"Listen, you music lovers can keep walking if you want," said Matty, "but right here is the subway downtown. Care to join us?"

We looked around, and we'd already come to the subway entrance. All the way downtown, I didn't want the ride to end. Lorraine and Sheila got off with us at the Times Square station. They had to take a different train, anyway. Matty and I walked them over to where they could board a train bound for their part of Brooklyn.

As the train came roaring into the station, it was me, not Matty, who wasn't cool. I grabbed Sheila and planted a big long kiss on her, right there. And I didn't give a darn who was looking, either. As she got on the train, I had this crazy impulse to get on, too. But then the doors shut.

As the train pulled away from the platform, she stood near the doors and gave me that great smile. Then, like she'd forgot, she looked panicked. It was too late to holler, so I pantomimed making a phone call. The last I saw was her smiling at me. I can still see her in that silly raincoat with the writing on it. I must have looked pretty shot down. Matty put his hand on my shoulder and said, "Cheer up, babe. We got some jazz to hear. You can call her tomorrow."

We went up the stairs and walked north on Broadway toward the "street." It was still pretty early for the jazz clubs to be starting up, so we had time to kill.

The only flick we hadn't seen was Tyrone Power in

Son of Fury at the Roxy. We looked over the still pictures and the sign boards outside, and decided to take a pass on it. It was one of those swordplay things.

It was only by accident we stumbled onto Charlie's Tavern. It was on Seventh Avenue between 51st and 52nd Streets, right near Roseland Ballroom, where Stan Kenton was playing. We had checked the times for Stan and discovered we were between shows, so we stopped into Charlie's for a beer. What a luck-out. Inside of the hour we were there, we saw half the musicians who were playing in town. Turned out that Charlie's was *the* place for musicians betwen shows or having a drink before going to work.

I first began to notice the musician customers when I saw this guy about five-foot-five, a white dude with his hair parted in the middle, like out of the '20's. He was carrying an odd-shaped trumpet case. Then I remembered where I'd seen him before. He was the only guy playing cornet in the Glenn Miller trumpet section. He was the one with the big solo on *String of Pearls.* I called the bartender over and pointed out the short guy with the cornet case.

"Didn't I see him with the Miller band at the Paramount today?" I asked.

"I guess you did, gate," smiled the bartender. "If you didn't see him, you sure heard him. That's Bobby Hackett."

Matty and I exchanged glances. Here was one of the guys from the swing era who played in the big time all the way into the '70's when he died. Hackett wasn't just a jazzman. He could also produce one of the sweetest ballad tones ever heard on a horn. But even when he played those creamy-dreamy solos in the '50's and '60's, you could still hear his hard jazz roots. It was his style that saved a lot of those dead-dog tunes and over-violined arrangements, like you hear on old folks' FM stations.

We had to do it. We went over and introduced our-

selves. He was sitting alone, and we talked for a few
minutes. He was very open and friendly, but he had a
personal reserve, like he knew he was top dog. And face
it, he was. What knocked me out was his speaking voice.
It seemed to come from the bottom of his shoes, it was so
deep. Sounded like he was using the voice of a dude
seven feet tall.

I was so flustered at meeting a real jazz great in person, that all the things I wanted to say or ask flew out of
my mind. Even Matty was at a loss for words. I also
realized that a lot of what I had to say to him wouldn't
have made sense. I knew about Bobby Hackett, but in a
historical way. I'd have been sure to screw up and ask
about things that might not have happened yet. So when
conversation flagged, we said so long and moved back to
where we'd been sitting.

It was a funny feeling. All the time we'd thought of
going back in time, we'd imagined talking with or meeting the great jazzmen. We never thought that when we
did, we'd have nothing to say. And we sure didn't. We
had another beer. After all, it was only a dime.

I checked our money supply, too. It didn't look all that
swift. We had a little over thirty-five dollars left. But I
didn't care too much. Tonight we were going to see and
hear the best, and Sunday . . . well, we'd deal with Sunday
when it came.

My main thought was to save enough out of what we
had, so I could take Sheila someplace. After that, I figured we'd start looking for that other Gate. I said as
much to Matty.

"Where do you think we can start?" he asked.

"I'm at a loss, man," I admitted. "I've been thinking
over what Pew said last night when we left. He said,
'Where the sea and the horizon change places and the
compass needle spins.' Now, I know I heard that description somewhere. Even before Abner Pew said it."

"You're right!" said Matty, snapping his fingers. "You heard it with me. Last fall. It was on that TV show . . ."

We both said it together: *"The Bermuda Triangle!"*

"That was it," Matty continued. "You remember when that flight of Navy planes disappeared, toward the end of the War? That was the radio message they sent back to the air base in Florida, just before they lost contact."

"And they never found even a piece of wreckage," I added. "Matty, do you think that's it?"

Matty pulled a glum face. "If it is, we got big trouble, bro."

"How so?"

"Well, how do you expect to get there? Nobody knows exactly where that flight of planes were when they disappeared. Even if we get to the coast of Florida, you saw yourself how huge that area they call the Triangle is. It took the navy three days of patrolling by air for the search. And they didn't even cover it all. Richie, I think we're screwed."

"Hold on, man," I said. "It doesn't have to be the only place where there's a Gate to the Future. Pew said that there were a bunch of locations."

"Fine," said Matty, still gloomy. "What if there's one in Italy, one in Germany and one in Japan? What do we do? Join the army and hope we get sent there to fight? Great, if we live. And face it, Richie, you don't really want to go back. You're goofy over that chick, and you don't have that much to lose back in 1976."

"Well, this is one fine time for you to start chickening out," I said.

"What kind of chickening out? I came, didn't I? I knew what could happen, didn't I? Maybe I wasn't thinking straight because of that hassle with my dad. I'm just saying I'm having second thoughts, that's all."

"Thanks a lot," I said sourly. "What's done is done. We're here, and it hasn't been all that bad, has it?"

"Only because we have bread. What happens when the money runs out?"

"We get jobs playing is what. Then when we get enough bread together, we go down to Florida and start scratching around."

"Swell," said Matty, "and what do we do for instruments? Can we buy a string bass and a drum set on what we've got? Come on, man. Admit it. You didn't think this trip out at all. You were so wound up with seeing and hearing the music, you didn't pay attention to basics. And you still won't. All you can think about is spending more money and that choir singer in Brooklyn, if she really is."

"Hey, wait a minute, man," I said, getting steamed. "You leave her out of it. And what do you mean, 'if she really is'?"

"You heard me, man, If she is. Come on. Do you think chicks are different because it's 1942? Chances are, they didn't even give us their real names. Sometimes, I think you got your head someplace else when it comes to chicks, Richie. First black chick you ever go out with, and right away it's *Love Story*. I never mentioned it to you, babe, but you got it in your mind that because the greatest jazzmen ever were black, everything black is great. It just ain't so. Having a black skin don't automatically make you sweet, pure, and a shining light. All it makes you is black, Jim. From there on, you're on your own."

"All right, man. If that's the way you feel about it."

"That's the way I feel about it."

I dug into my pocket and took out the remaining cash we had. I split it up the middle and slid it across the bar to him. He knew what I meant. If he wanted to split up, he could walk anytime. Without another word, Matty picked up the money on the bar and walked out of Charlie's. He turned at the corner, and I watched him cross Seventh Avenue toward where the jazz clubs were. I wanted to call out and stop him, but be flogged if I would. I sat at the bar, staring at my half-finished beer and Matty's. I reached over and poured what was left into my glass. I had seventeen dollars left, and Matty was right, even if I hadn't liked the way he said it. No point in wasting even a half glass of a ten-cent beer. I felt more alone than I'd ever been in my entire life.

8

Street of Dreams

I sat there in Charlie's in a state of funk. Maybe Matty had been right all down the line. I've never felt like I really belonged anywhere since Harry and Mom broke up. Even before then, when they were on the outs.

I guess the whole thing about living in the 1940's was an escape from facing up to a 1976 I didn't make or care too much for. I had jumped at the chance to go back when Pew told us about the Gate because I just plain didn't care if I came back or not. But I have to admit, I had talked Matty into it. If he hadn't had the fight with his old man, he wouldn't have gone. I know it. He wouldn't even have had the fight if he hadn't been out with me on his birthday.

And I hadn't planned much of anything after seeing 52nd Street in its heyday. When Matty had talked about geting jobs with no instruments, it had hit home hard. To buy any decent kind of ax would take a lot more than we had together. And there was no question of doing any other kind of work. I hadn't told Matty, but even that was out. We had no I.D. for 1942. My wallet had cards in it that gave my birthdate as thirty-four years from now. Every male citizen my age in 1942 had a draft card. We couldn't get jobs long enough to buy instruments. But maybe . . . I had it!

We'd never talked about pawnshops. If Matty and I pooled the bread we had left, we could maybe get a cheap bass at a pawnshop. Drums were too expensive, but I've played on Kay plywood basses made in the '40's. They're good, serviceable instruments. And they weren't expensive even in the '40's. Yeah, it just maybe could be done! I snapped out of it quick. I had to find Matty before he spent any money. We just yet might be able to do it. Problem was, where did Matty go to?

I looked at the clock behind the bar that advertised Trommer's White Label beer. It read 9:15. I asked the bartender if it was the right time.

"Nah," he said, "that's bar time. Ten minutes fast. The cops are tough on closing time at 4:00 A.M. If you ever tried to turn off a whole bar full of cats after work, you know it can't be done that quick. So we set the clock fast and call last round early. It's still a problem, though. Why? You gotta be some place to play tonight?"

I was flattered. The bartender had asumed Matty and I were working musicians. I maybe would have let him go on thinking it, just for fun, but that wouldn't have told me what I wanted to know.

"No, not tonight. My buddy and I are from the Island. Came in to catch the band at Kelly's Stable."

"Oh. The Sabby Lewis Band or the King Cole Trio?"

"Both. Do you know when they start up?"

"Right now, kiddo. But you ain't gonna see either one this time of night. The Pete Brown Quartet opens the night. Then King Cole and after them, the Sabby Lewis Band."

"Who's Pete Brown?"

"Alto player. Big, heavy, colored cat. He was here while you and your friend was talkin' with Bobby Hackett. Left while you and the colored kid was havin' words. Want another beer?"

"What time should Nat Cole be on at Kelly's?"

"Oh, you know him, then. His friends call him Nat. He should go on . . . um, around ten, ten-fifteen."

"Then I'll have another beer."

I'd made a goof. Cole didn't call himself Nat until after the trio broke up. But this bartender knew a lot that could help me. I had to try for some information. It was worth the dime, so I bought the barman a beer. Soon as I offered, he smiled and stuck his hand out.

"Jimmy Nelson," he said, shaking my hand. "I'm filling in today for the regular man. What's your ax?"

"Richie Gilroy. Bass."

"No kiddin'? I'm a doghouse man myself. Tryin' to raise a little mazuma so I can get it outa hock."

"Then maybe you can help me. I want to get a line on a good, cheap, uh, doghouse," I said, using Jimmy Nelson's term for a bass. Actually, when you look at a bass in a hard case, it does look like some kind of little building the size of a doghouse.

"Did you try the hock shops around the corner on Eighth Avenue?"

"Not yet."

"Your best bet. Hit 'em first thing Monday morning. Lotsa guys who play on weekends put 'em in on Monday and take 'em out on Friday. That way, they got walkin'-around money. You catch some gate who's down on his luck, you could probably make a good deal. How much you wanta spend?"

"About thirty bucks."

"No good. You can't get anything but crap for that. Maybe a plywood in bad shape."

"A plywood would be just fine," I said, thinking of the old Kays.

"Is that all?" said Jimmy Nelson. "I got a beat-up old plywood back in the liquor room. Some cat left it for his bar tab one night. He never came back. But it ain't mine to sell. You'd haveta see the owner."

"Is it playable?" I asked.

"You betcha," said Jimmy Nelson. "I used it two weeks ago. The owner lent it to me for the job. It's no great instrument, but you could work with it. At least I did."

"Any idea what he wants for it?"

"You're talkin' in the right neighborhood when you said thirty bucks."

"Great!" I said. "I'll be back in a few hours. I have to find my friend. Tell the owner I want that bass!"

"Don't worry, kiddo," said Jimmy Nelson. "It's been here for a year, now. It ain't gonna run away."

I picked up my change and left a dime for Nelson. Then I took off for Kelly's Stable. I was sure Matty would show there eventually. We had planned our night around it. Even mad as he was, Matty wouldn't have missed that show, I knew.

By two in the morning, I wasn't so sure. I'd sat through two complete shows by the three groups on the bill at Kelly's, and no Matty Owen. But I must admit that if I was going to wait anywhere, I was in a great place for it.

Nat Cole was fantastic. It took some getting used to, hearing group vocals from the Trio. I didn't know the other guys sang, too. I hadn't realized, either, what a truly fine pianist Nat Cole was. He played a lot like he sang on the up-tempo numbers. He'd hang behind the beat and play short, economical phrases. But so well thought out.

His bass player was Wesley Prince back then. He was a thin man with long thin fingers that flew over the bass. After two sets of watching him, I wasn't too sure I could even get a job playing in this town. Oscar Moore, Nat's guitarist, looked like a black Buddha. When he played, all that moved was his hands. But, oh, the sounds that came out!

It was getting harder and harder for me to concentrate on the music, even when the big Sabby Lewis Band came out. I was taken back when they did. I had heard that the band was mixed, racially. If you can call one white dude in a black band a mix, that was it. He played the heavy tenor sax solos. So I knew who he had to be. It was Jerry Hefron, the guy who also did a lot of arranging. I thought about what Matty had said about my thing for black being better. Well, here was a white dude doing more than just holding his own in a black band. And, babe, did they blow! They had a female vocalist who doubled on accordion, if you're ready for that. I didn't get her name. But she was worth the trip all by herself.

The middle of Nat Cole's second set, he went into *Sweet Lorraine*, which right away made me think of Sheila and Lorraine. It was getting me down. I couldn't take too much more waiting, so I drifted out onto the "street" after Nat finished. I had to locate Matty.

I must have hit every joint, good and bad, on 52nd Street. No go. I should have known. I walked back toward Charlie's, thinking Matty might have looked for me there. I almost walked right by the place, but I heard the sounds.

I hadn't seen it before because it was upstairs. There was a doorway with a sign that said HORN OF PLENTY. Under that, hand lettered, was a sign that read JAM SESION TONIGHT. (9:00 P.M. TO?). Somebody at the Horn of Plenty wasn't a very swift speller. It was the only joint I hadn't tried, so I went upstairs.

It was a very small club. I don't think you could have put more than fifty people in it. Even then, you'd have to make room for the smoke that was so thick in the air you could chew it. I smelled some smoke that wasn't strictly out of a green Lucky Strike pack, too. All the tiny tables were full, and I went to the six-foot-long bar and started to order a beer.

The room was L-shaped, with the band around the bend, so you couldn't see the far corner of the bandstand.

The group playing wasn't bad. They weren't great, either. But then, again, I had come from hearing the very best all day. Maybe my point of view was out of whack. The tenor sax player had just finished a some-what undistinguished solo on *I Can't Give You Anything But Love,* and the drummer took his solo. Soon as I heard him, I jumped to my feet and craned my neck around the bend. And there, sitting at the drums, smiling like he'd found a friend and playing his ass off, was Matthew Oscar Owen!

The number ended, and the tenor player stepped to the microphone. He was a tall, thin black man with a tuxedo on. The tux may have started out even blacker than its wearer, but evidently both were over the hill. The tux was threadbare and had a vague, green, moldy sheen. When the tenor man smiled, I could see he was missing a couple of crucial teeth. Which probably explained his breathy tone when he played.

"Ladees and gennulmen," he intoned, "we are gonna take a brief pause for the cause, but we'll be back with more of the tunes that makes you gates and chicks swing! We'd like you to thank our guest drummer, who did so fine. Let's hear a big hand for Matty Owen!"

The house broke into some raggedy applause, and Matty stood up and bowed. When he did, I caught his eye. I guess he was over his mad, because he gave me a big grin and waved me over to the bandstand. I got there just as he was stepping down. We both started talking at once.

"I got a job!" he said at the same time I said, "I found a bass!"

We backed off and tried again. Matty sure enough had a job. For the night, anyway. The regular drummer hadn't shown up. Matty sat in and, after one set, the tenor sax player had asked him to stay for the rest of the night.

"How much is he paying?" I asked, thinking of the bass for sale.

"MMMrblegrmf," said Matty.

"What did you say?" I asked. Matty looked very sheepish, then said it so I could understand.

"Ten bucks," he said. "But that's only for a start," he added hurriedly. "If Johnny fires the drummer, I got his gig for seventy a week."

"Who's Johnny, the tenor man?"

"Yeah. Pretty poor, huh?"

"You said it. I didn't."

Matty smiled and put his arm over my shoulder. We walked toward the front of the room. I thought we were headed for the bar, but he steered me to a door alongside the men's room that was marked KEEP OUT: EMPLOYEES ONLY. It was a dressing room for the musicians. There were only two of them inside, the tenor man and the bass player. Matty introduced me to Johnny Rogers, the tenor player/leader, and to Ollie Phillips, the white bass player, and only paleface in the band. We said the usual things you have to say to guys when even they know it was mediocre. Matty took Rogers aside and whispered something. He looked over at me, nodded, then he and Ollie Phillips split.

I sat down on a rickety chair, and Matty sprawled out on a couch that looked like George Washington had refused to sleep on.

"Before you say anything, Richie," said Matty from the couch, "I want to say I'm sorry about what I said. I was down, man. I thought we were completely screwed.

But I walked right into this job, like nothing at all."

"Is it Union?" I asked.

"Are you out of your tree? Where would I get a Union card for 1942? This joint is as close to Union as I am to Snow White, baby. But it's bread, and don't forget it. What's this, you got a bass?"

I explained what had happened at Charlie's after Matty had left, and I told him where I'd looked for him.

"I'll be . . ." he said, smiling ruefully. "Here I been workin' my buns off, and you been hanging out digging the sounds."

"So you say," I came back. "I was looking for you."

"Groovy," he laughed. "Next time you're missing, I think I'll look for you on the French Riviera. No telling when those broads in the bikinis might stop passing, and you'd drop in."

"You forgetting that the only dudes on the Riviera right now speak German, man?"

"You know, you're right? I was forgetting. Somehow it doesn't seem as though there's a war going on."

"That was my mistake, Matt. The war is only two months old today. It was on December 7th they bombed Pearl Harbor. The U.S.A isn't really in it full scale yet. Right now, in New York, it's like it's all so far away. Nobody I talked to says much about it, either. Wonder why?"

"I picked up a newspaper," Matty said. "I think it's because the government hasn't released any casualty figures or lists yet. If you don't know folks are dying, you can't get worked up about it."

"I guess you're right. But Matty, I meant to ask you. Whose drums are you gonna play on if you do get this job?"

"The ones out there. Johnny owns them. The prices he pays his sidemen, they could as easy not show. He bought them when his last drummer showed up for work and said the drum set was in hock. Johnny fired the drummer. And because he knew the dude was broke, he bought the pawn ticket from the guy for a night's pay."

"Sweet guy."

"I don't have to love the dude, just work for him," said Matty. "Hey, listen. I'm due back onstage soon. Tell you what. You sit at that little table for two right in front of the drums. That's the last place they sit anyone down, 'cause of the noise. I have three more sets to play. Nurse a beer as long as you can."

"Three more sets?" I gasped. "It's two in the morning now. How many do you have to do for ten bucks?"

"It's not that bad," Matty explained. "The house band only really works until about now. The guys playing on the 'street' come in after two, and they sit in. Soon as a guest drummer comes in, I lay out. I'm sort of a standby drummer after 2:00 A.M. That's how Johnny gets away with non-Union wages. If anybody from the Union comes by, he says everyone on stage but him is a guest. He's got the only contract in the house."

"I was wondering how it worked," I said. "What a ripoff."

"Beats no gig at all, don't it?" said Matty. And he was right.

I settled down at the tiny table near the drums and ordered a beer. The place was full already, and the tables were so close together, I could have reached over and touched either of the two guys sitting at the table nearest me.

They were an unlikely pair of jazz fans. They both wore clothes that were more out of the '20's or '30's than the "now" of 1942. One was about thirty, dark haired and built like a wrestler. The other dude was easy in his sixties and was wearing a three-piece suit with a wing collar. He had a walking stick with a silver handle at the side of his chair. He was almost completely bald except

for a fringe of silver hair that he wore long, for 1942.
Almost reached his collar.

The music began, and I turned to watch the action at
the bandstand. The table really was too close to the drums.
So I wouldn't get blasted, I turned my head away from
the bandstand, and it ended up I was almost facing the
two odd-looking dudes. It didn't make any difference to
them that the band was on. They kept on with what
seemed to be a nonstop conversation. They were talking
in low voices, their heads close together. I was only
inches away, but I couldn't hear a word.

The band went into an up-tempo version of *Honey-
suckle Rose*, and I let my mind wander to plans for tomorrow and the search for the Future Gate. But any
time the level of sound onstage dropped, I could still
hear them running on. I couldn't help wonder what was
so important that they would come all the way to a jazz
joint, then talk all through the music. I kept getting
snatches of conversation in the lulls. Then all of a sudden, my ears perked up.

"*Der neue Brandstifter . . .*" said the heavyset guy.

"In English, you fool!" snapped the old dude, spotting
me watching.

It was all I heard for a while. They turned away from
me and the bandstand, too. It was hard to do, but they
got their heads even closer together. I tried to pick up
more. Once in a few measures, I'd heard more.

"Your pickup has been arranged at . . ." from the old
guy. Then later, "Yes, I'm certain. The car will be ready,
ja?" from the young guy.

Just then, another man joined the fun couple at the
table. He was young, blond, over six feet. He looked like
an ad for a ski resort. Even to the heavy suntan he had. I
wondered where he got it in New York in February.
They all settled down then and, ignoring the band, put

their heads together. I couldn't get what they were saying, but I didn't have too much doubt as to what they were.

I knew from my studies that the Germans had landed spies in New York in the early months of the war. These guys were actually plotting right next to me! And it was a smart thing they were doing.

Jazz fans are the easiest people in the world to get along with. If you don't bug them, or make noise when they're trying to hear, they couldn't care less if you had two heads. The loud band in the Horn of Plenty covered any conversation. And what's the last place you'd look for a spy? In a jazz place, natch. Jazz is so American, no one'd think of a foreigner going to hear it. In 1942, anyway.

The band clattered through the last bars of *Amapola*, with Johnny Rogers losing badly to the Jimmy Dorsey solo. Evidently, a guest drummer had come in. Matty was giving up his chair onstage. He joined me at the tiny table.

I filled him in on what I thought was taking place at the next table over. Matty was cool and didn't look directly at them. He copped a sneaky look when he could. He moved opposite me and leaned back in his chair. That way, he was almost part of the party alongside us. After a few minute's listen, he motioned me toward the dressing room.

Once we were inside, Matty said, "You're right, Richie. Those dudes are spies, all right. I heard more than you could. I was right on top of them. They've got something big going, too."

"What do you suppose it is?"

"Couldn't say. But one of them doesn't have too much English. If my German was better, I could tell you more. But I know they're for sure spies."

"How can you tell?"

"I heard one of them mention *unterseeboot*. That's German for a submarine. And I heard the dude with bad English say *brandstifter* and that clinched it."

"What's that mean?"

Matty gave me a sickish look. "It means fire bomb, babe. I remember the word from German class. We read about what the Allies did to Dresden in 1944. These dudes are out to blow something up. Something big at that."

My heart sank. I mean, I'm as patriotic as the next guy in 1976. But this was a different story. These were the bad guys, no mistake, and they were going to do something that could cost lives!

"We gotta turn them in," I said.

"Sure," said Matty. "We just bust into the local FBI office, wherever that is, and say, 'Hi there! I'm from the year 1976, and I want to report some German saboteurs.' How far do you think we'll get? I say leave 'em alone, Richie. We got enough problems now."

"We gotta turn them in, Matty."

Matty plumped down on the ratty couch so hard that dust rose. He breathed out heavily.

"Richie, you got to face some facts," he said. "First off, we don't have a shred of hard proof. Yeah, I overheard what I heard. But I don't speak German any better than you speak French. I could be wrong . . ."

"Wait a minute," I cut in. "You said that you were convinced."

"I am, I am. But I'm saying that what I've heard isn't enough to go and blow the whistle on these guys with. And we can't notify anyone. The first thing any fuzz will ask for is our I.D., and baby, we ain't got any."

"We could give an anonymous tip on the phone," I said.

"Swell. Is the FBI open twenty-four hours a day? Do you know where they are? What's the phone number?

And do you think they'll follow up before these guys leave this joint? It's closing time soon. Get real, Richie. We got to give this counterspy thing a pass."

"We could follow them and see where they go, then call the cops," I said.

Matty sighed heavily again.

"OK, OK. If they leave, and I'm saying *if*, before the joint closes, I'm staying here. The leader owes me ten bucks. If they wait until I knock off, we follow them. Fair enough?"

"Fair enough," I said. "But we gotta . . ."

"Yeah, I know. We gotta turn them in."

I don't know what kind of luck you'd call it, now that I look back. But the three guys didn't leave until after closing. They were the last people out the door, and they were still rapping as they went. Matty and I waited for a ten count, then followed them out into the street. We got downstairs just in time to see the old guy getting into a cab. I wasn't close enough to hear the address he gave to the driver. The other two guys, the young ones, were walking over toward the East Side. Matty and I tagged along.

"Do you think they're suspicious?" I asked as we walked behind them, about a half block, on the opposite side of the street.

"Don't see why they should be," said Matty. "We left the club the same time as they did. We could just as easy be going where they're going. Or at least in the same direction for a few blocks."

The two young spies walked over as far as Third Avenue and got on the El on the uptown side. There weren't too many people around. It was close to 4:00 A.M. But there were enough folks going home, or someplace, to have ten or twelve people waiting on the platform. Matty and I tried to look as cool as possible.

When the train thundered up to the platform, we got

in the car next to the spies. I stood at the space between cars and glanced into the car ahead. They were talking again. I don't know if he really noticed me, but the heavyset, dark-haired guy looked up for a second and our eyes met. I got a chill. This dude had the meanest set of blue eyes I've ever seen, in or out of flicks.

If he had spotted me, he didn't let on. He just went back to the nonstop rap he'd been having with the heavyset guy all night. I told Matty I thought I might have tipped them.

"No way to tell," he said. "I feel dumb about this, too. What if these guys are just German-Americans?"

"You changing your mind on me?"

"No, no. But I was thinking. They could be perfectly all right. My German is so bad, they could have been talking about war news or something when they mentioned a fire bomb, that's all."

"Do you really think that?"

"No, I don't, Richie. But can't you see? We could be on a silly wild goose chase. We got plenty of grief the way it is. We could have trouble with the fuzz over this, too."

"All right, all right," I grumbled. "We'll just see where they go, and when we do we'll . . . Hey, let's go. They're getting off!"

When the doors opened for the East 86th Street station, they hadn't moved at all. At the last minute, they jumped to their feet like on cue, and slid out between the closing doors. Matty and I made it at the last possible second. But we were the only ones besides the two spies who had gotten off the train at 86th Street. We were nearer to the stairs to the street than they were. But there wasn't any doubt that the two guys were on to us.

They were about thirty feet away. They said something to each other, then they started walking toward us.

They weren't hurrying, but there wasn't the slightest doubt that they were after us.

"Matty?" I whispered.

"Yeah?"

"Ready to run?" I asked.

"Oh, I wouldn't do that, were I you," said a voice from behind us.

I spun around. So did Matty. The old dude from the club stood behind us. He was wearing a topcoat and a Homburg hat. He still carried his walking stick, but now it was in two pieces. One piece he held lightly in his left hand, like an umbrella case. The other was in his right hand. But where the silver handle should have met the wood of the stick, the handle ended in a nasty blade about two feet long. And it was pointed straight at my navel!

9

Spies, Spies!

"Once again, young man," said the old guy, "what is your name?"

"I told you a hundred times," said Matty.

"Then tell me again," said the old guy.

"Matthew Owen," said Matty wearily. "I live at 225 Cedar Street in Branford, Long Island. I'm a student."

I think it had been more than a hundred times Matty and I had told our story to the old guy. We were both sitting in old-timey kitchen chairs in an apartment on East 88th Street. We were tied to the chairs with electrical wiring cord. The old guy had been questioning us on and off since the night before. The ski instructor dude had left. I wasn't sure what time it was, but even through the drawn curtains, I could see the sun was in a position that indicated about noon.

They had brought us here from the 86th Street El station at 4:00 A.M. It meant we'd been questioned for eight hours. Neither Matty nor I had gotten any sleep.

And we'd thought we were so swift, tailing the Germans. The old guy had thought it amusing what amateurs we'd been. He'd been on to us from the start, at the club, when he noticed me listening in on their conversation. When he'd left the club in the taxi, all he'd done was ride around the block to make sure his two buddies weren't being tailed. When he saw us following the two of them, he just got out of the cab and followed us. We were so involved in not being seen by the other two, we never looked to see if *we* were being followed!

The Germans had taken turns questioning us through the night. Matty was continuing his recitation.

"I'm due to graduate from Branford High this June. My father is James Owen. He's an electronic parts salesman. The firm is Eastern Elec——."

The old guy had interrupted Matty with a ringing slap to the face. I winced at the sound. I'd collected my share of those over the past eight hours, too. Matty was lucky. The old guy didn't hit like Ski Instructor did. But it still wasn't too much fun, no matter who was doing it.

In a way, we lucked out. Once the old guy saw the I.D. I had in my wallet with a birth date of 1959, the questioning had begun with no fooling around. He didn't believe it, of course. He thought that we had some sort of coded I.D. and were government agents. At first, we'd tried not to say anything about how we'd gotten to New York in 1942. But I'll tell you something about interrogation. After a while, you talk.

Oh sure, I've seen the spy flicks, where they work some dude over. He grits his teeth and tells them to buzz off. Man, that's all built on the idea that you've teeth left. After my first few backhanded slaps from Ski Instructor, my head was ringing. By the time he finished the second session, I was singing like a bird. I'm ashamed to admit it, but I'm just not the hero type. They didn't have to take out any spooky equipment and work any exotic tortures on me. Plain old-fashioned hitting did the trick.

When it started, I held out for the first session, mostly because I was afraid of looking chicken in front of Matty. But after the first slapping around, they kept Matty in the back room while they questioned me, and did the same with me when they interrogated Matty. When the second time in the kitchen chair came around for me, I was relieved when they told me Matty had talked. All they needed from me was details. I spilled my guts.

I had no way of knowing that Matty hadn't talked. They were keeping us separated. I felt somewhat better when they pulled the same trick on Matty, and he had talked, too. After that, they kept us together in the back room of this tiny, three-room apartment. But it didn't make any difference that we had told it all, right from Abner Pew on down. They didn't believe that, either. And they wouldn't stop the questioning and hitting. I was at the end of my rope. I was ready to tell them I was the Queen of the May, if it would stop the hitting.

This last session with the heavyset guy and the old guy, they had me watch while they knocked Matty around. It was just a matter of time before my turn was due. I wasn't eager for it, either.

The old guy was continuing, "And this so-called gate. Where is it located?"

"I don't know," said Matty, desperately. "Don't you understand? I just don't know. Can't you leave me alone?" The old guy slapped Matty again, backhand and forehand, two or three times, real fast.

"Can't you see we're telling the truth?" I hollered. "Let him alone."

The old guy turned to me with a smile that turned my stomach.

"Ah, young Mr. Gilroy," he grinned, wickedly. "Your

solicitude for your friend is touching. Perhaps you would care to take his place?"

I didn't say anything to that. I knew too well it was my turn coming up, anyway. I was getting mentally prepared for it, when the phone rang. The old guy picked it up after it rang four times, stopped, then rang again a few seconds later. He spoke quickly in German. It could have been Chinese so far as I was concerned. All I got were the *jas, neins* and the *guts*.

The old guy was really into his rap when the heavyset guy made some motions toward us, and asked him something in German. The old guy glanced at us where we were sitting and smiled. Then he said something in German. The heavyset dude nodded. I looked over at Matty. He reacted like he'd been whammed in the head by Ski Instructor.

The old guy hung up the phone and turned to face us. He must have gotten some kind of hurry up message on the phone. He began rapping orders at the heavyset guy, who came over and stood behind my chair. I felt queasy in the stomach.

In those flicks I'd seen, this is where the heavy dude comes up behind the chair and does in the guy they're questioning. When his arms went around me from behind, I let out a little moan, and I'm embarrassed to admit it, I pissed in my pants. Don't laugh at that if you've never been so sure you were going to die in a very nasty way!

To my immense relief, the heavyset guy picked both me and the chair up and walked me into the back room. In a second, he was back carrying Matty the same way. It might have given you an idea how scary things were to see this bruiser pick us both up that way. Both Matty and I are over six foot, and we weigh about 170 pounds each. He shut the door to the back room without turning on the light.

The room we were in was tiny. The only light that came in was a slice of gray daylight from the one window in the room. It faced on an air shaft. If you don't know what an air shaft is, you've probably never been in a New York tenement building. Not that you've missed much. An air shaft is just what it sounds like. A hole in the center of a building that has little windows facing it. Its only purpose is to let in light and air for the back rooms of apartments that wouldn't get any otherwise.

I could tell from being able to see a little piece of sky through the filth-encrusted window that we were on a top floor. I'd seen the building when we got shuffled in at knife point. It was five floors high, and a long way down from the air shaft window. I waited until I was sure the heavy bruiser wasn't coming back in. I could hear him rapping in German with the old guy in the kitchen.

I whispered to Matty, "You OK, man?"

"I'm alive," he said gloomily. "That bastard shook my tooth loose."

Matty has a false tooth in front. He lost the real one in an accident playing ball. I guess the old guy packed some wallop when he wanted to. Or he was doing a special number on Matty on account of Matty being black. He had kept calling Matty by the name Owens instead of Owen. Jesse Owens was the Black athlete that had made a monkey out of Hitler's boys at the 1936 Berlin Olympics in track. Evidently, Nazis don't forget easy.

"Listen," I said. "Did you understand any of what they were saying in the kitchen?"

"Not too much, Richie," whispered Matty. "It isn't like school. They rattle away way too fast for me to get more than one word in five." Matty squirmed around in his chair to face me a little. "And Strong Boy speaks some accent or dialect I can hardly understand."

"Do you know why they stopped questioning us all of a sudden?" I asked.

Matty looked even gloomier and squirmed around in the chair again. It was a bit rickety, and I was afraid the two in the kitchen would hear it. We both sat quietly for a while until we could hear conversation resume in the kitchen. Matty broke the silence.

"Yeah, I got that. The old guy—the bruiser calls him Colonel, by the way—got some hot flash from the higher-ups. He speaks beautiful German. I get most of what he says, if he ain't talking too fast."

"Well, for God's sake," I hissed, "tell me what's going on!"

Matty took a deep breath, then said in a matter-of-fact tone, "The Colonel told Strong Boy that he's got to leave. Whatever it is that they're up to, it's gonna happen real soon. He told the muscle to question us again in two hours, then again in another two."

"Jeez," I moaned. "Again? I can't take too much more."

"Don't worry," said Matty in the same flat voice. "You don't have to. The Colonel told Strong Boy that if he doesn't get any answers the second time, he's supposed to kill us."

My stomach sank to somewhere around my ankles.

"My God! What are we going to do, Matt?" I said.

"Well, unless you know something I don't, babe," said Matty, "I think what we're going to do is die."

We sat in silence so thick you could chew it for some time. I nearly jumped out of my skin when the phone rang in the other room. I could hear the Colonel on the horn. He sounded excited. Then he began to shout. I knew it had to be serious. He hadn't raised his voice above conversational level all through the questioning. There was some scraping of chairs, and Strong Boy came in. I tried to make myself as small as possible in the chair I was tied to. But he walked right over to Matty.

I thought to myself, "Here we go. This is the end." I think I started to cry a little. I'm not sure. I nearly died of relief when he didn't grab Matty by the throat or anything. He was only tightening the wires that held us fast. He checked out my tie-up and then faced us, standing in the doorway to the kitchen.

I saw the Colonel, his coat and hat on, go out the door. He stopped at the last minute and said something in German to Strong Boy, who nodded and said *ja wohl*, just like in the movies. Then he left.

The bruiser regarded us with an evil look and said in heavily accented English, "Vell, boys. Ve must too soon part. I come back in a little time, and ve vill talk again. Then you may be free to go, *gut?*"

The bastard! He didn't know we understood what was really going to happen to us. I wasn't about to give him the satisfaction of thinking we were that dumb. I was going to say something, then I changed my mind. Instead I said, "We'll be here."

It broke up the big moose. He laughed like mad and said, "Oh, *ja*, you vill be here." Then, still laughing, he left the room, closing the door behind him.

In a minute, we heard the front door open. We couldn't tell, but it sounded like Strong Boy was splitting. I mean, we didn't hear anyone come in, and Strong Boy wasn't talking to anyone. We waited until it was very quiet, then began to holler. It was taking a chance, I know. Strong Boy had a short fuse. But when we got no response from the front room, we were pretty sure he had gone out.

But holler as we might, it didn't get any reaction from outside the apartment, either. It may have been that there was no one else living on the floor we were on. After we started getting hoarse, we knocked off the shouting. Matty looked at me from his chair.

"I think we're wasting time, Richie," he said. "That goon is going to be back any minute, now. Bounce your chair over here. I want to try something."

"What?"

"Never mind. Just get over here. If it works, you'll know soon enough." .

I managed to slide my chair most of the way over to Matty. Then I hit a rise in the uncovered wood floor. The chair tipped, and I fell at Matty's feet, facing away from him. I could hear him squirming around in his chair. The old piece of furniture was complaining mightily.

"Now," said Matty, "if I can only . . . hold still, Richie."

I felt a terrible blow, right in the small of my back, it seemed. It hurt as bad as the Ski Instructor.

"What are you doing, man?" I shouted. I got another shot in the low back for an answer.

"These chairs are so rickety that the wires give way a little when you work on them," grunted Matty, as he gave me another bone-jarring kick. "I've got one foot and my leg loose. If I can get the right angle to kick from, I can bust up the chair, and you'll be loose. Maybe those lessons at the *dojo* weren't a waste of time after all."

It dawned on me what Matty meant, and what the kicks were. He had gone to a *dojo* to study karate a few years ago. But he'd dropped out after six months. Didn't care for the idea of busting up people and bricks, he'd said.

Karate or not, he was right about the chairs not being strong. With one last kick that rattled my teeth, the chair back splintered. I wriggled free and in a few seconds, we were both loose. But we could barely stand up, or use our hands. We'd been tied up for so long, it took us precious minutes to get our circulation going. It hurt like crazy, too.

Soon as we could move, we went into the kitchen. It was empty except for the two remaining chairs, an enamel-topped table and some dirty coffee cups on the

table. No sign of Strong Boy. But the door to the hall was
locked with one of those police locks that has a steel rod
sunk into the floor. And there was a keylock on the
inside of the lock as well as the outside. We'd gotten out
of the chairs, but we were still locked up just as se-
curely. We could maybe have broken down the door
itself, using the kitchen table for a battering ram. But
we had no idea when the muscleman was coming back.
Or if he was going to be alone when he did. Or have
a gun or knife. There was no question in my mind that
the two of us couldn't take him. Not after he had picked
us up like stuffed dolls earlier. I walked back into the
room where we'd been tied up and opened the air shaft
window. It hadn't been opened in years, I could tell.
I looked down. A five-floor drop. No help. Then I
looked up.

By craning my neck, I could see the edge of the roof
above the air shaft window. It was no more than a foot
and a half above the top of the window frame. I hiked
myself up onto the inside sill, and squirmed through the
narrow window until I was sitting on the outside sill with
my legs inside the room. The outside sill was no more
than three inches wide. No way to stand on it without
falling. There wasn't anything out there to hang on to.
But if Matty held my ankles and legs fast from inside, I
could maybe reach the roof edge and pull myself up.
Then if I took the electrical wiring cord that we'd been
tied with, I could drop it down to Matty and pull him up!
I was about to call him, when I heard this thumping from
the kitchen. I rushed in.

Matty had the leg from the chair he'd kicked to pieces
and was doing what we should have thought of from the
first. He was knocking the hinge pins out of their settings
on the door. They were encrusted with years of old paint,
but he'd already got one of them out and the second one

was loose! The police lock only stopped the door from swinging open on its hinges. With the pins loose, we lifted the entire door out of the frame and with a clatter and some dust, we were into the outside hall of the apartment building!

We raced to the head of the stairs and started down for the street. We got three steps down when I peered over the open stairwell and spotted Strong Boy and Ski Instructor coming up. I pulled my head back fast and grabbed Matty by the arm, putting my hand over his mouth, so he wouldn't cry out. I showed him the two goons on the way up.

We ran to the roof stairs. From the foot of the flight, we could see the padlock on the inside of the door.

"Come on, man," I hissed to Matty. "Back into the place!"

The footsteps on the stairs were getting closer. I could hear Ski Instructor and Strong Boy rapping in German. I told Matty my plan, and in a few seconds, I was hanging by my fingertips, five floors above the street, hoping to God that the section of rain gutter I was hanging on to wouldn't let go. Blessedly, it held, and I dropped the cord down to Matty.

I grabbed hold of a chimney nearby and wrapped the wire around my waist. There wasn't enough slack to tie it around the chimney itself. When Matty swung his weight on the line, I thought the narrow wire was going to cut me in half. But we both held. I pulled him over the edge. We never bothered to look back.

We took off over the roofs of the row houses and pulled desperately on each roof door. They were all locked, but one of them pulled open with a rending sound. We half ran, half fell down the stairs to the street, and took off running for Third Avenue. We didn't stop or say a word to each other until we were both on an El train headed midtown. Even then, we just looked at each other and grinned from relief.

If I had known it then, I would have enjoyed it more. It was just about the last hassle-free time we spent for the next twenty-four hours!

10

I Don't Want to
Set the World on Fire

I glanced around the car. People were staring at us. I couldn't blame them, either. Here it was the middle of winter, and we were both in shirt-sleeves and covered with the filth from the roof and air shaft. Matty's face was puffy and bruised, and I'm sure I looked just as bad from the beatings we'd taken. Feeling like myself for the first time in what seemed like years, I said to Matty, "Hey, man, why don't you clean up your act? Folks are staring."

Matty roared in laughter, and more heads swiveled around to look at us.

"At least I don't pee in my pants, junior," he smirked and pointed to my soggy trousers. In the excitement, I'd forgotten about it. I must have really looked like something else. We joked and goofed on each other until we got off the El.

Our clothes were a problem, for sure. Lucky it wasn't

a very cold day. Even so, it was no joke being in shirt-sleeves in forty-degree weather. We had to get topcoats somewhere. But where? It was Sunday, and all the used clothing stores and pawnshops under the El were closed. I guess God has mercy on drunks and fools, like Harry says. We found a place off Third Avenue and 14th Street. It was run by an old Jewish dude with a beard. We got two coats for seven-and-a-half bucks. And the only reason we had money to pay for them was that Matty had stashed his ten dollars from the Horn of Plenty in his shoe. The Nazis had gotten our remaining silver dollars when they'd searched us. Even worse, they'd taken my iron key to the Future Gate.

The coat I got smelled like it had been owned by a guy whose deodorant had quit about a year before he sold the coat. Or else he died in it. Matty's was less fragrant, but the sleeves ended four inches above his wrists. I'm sure we made some picture. I glanced at a street clock. It read almost 4:30. Then it hit me. I hadn't called Sheila!

Matty and I ducked into a Bickford's restaurant, which was a fast-food chain. We got two cups of coffee, and I got some nickels and headed for the telephone. It rang and rang. I was ready to hang up when someone finally answered.

"Hallo?"

"Hello," I said. "Could you please call Sheila to the phone?"

"Sheila who?" asked the voice. "Ain't no Sheila here."

"Is this HE 3–5649?"

"Yeah, it is. But there ain't no Sheila here. This here is Brooklyn Eye and Ear Hospital. Somebody's pulling your leg, buddy."

I hung up and walked back to the table where Matty was sitting, nursing his cup of coffee. He looked up as I sat down and said, "What's the word? She gonna meet you?"

I told him what had happened when I called the number Sheila gave me. I must say, he didn't rub it in. He just nodded and said, "Well, that's the way it be's sometime, bro."

"I'm sorry, man," I said after we sat silent for a while.

"Nothing to say, Richie," Matty said.

"Ah, yes, there is. We nearly split up because of me being hung up on that chick. And none of the other things would have happened if we hadn't split up. Maybe I'm a jinx, Matt."

Matty stirred his coffee and looked out the window at the street. Then he smiled widely.

"No way, kid," he laughed. "Don't you know that black cats are a jinx? It's probably me! Come on, let's have something hot. I want to get over to the Horn of Plenty and see if I for sure have that gig."

"Matty!" I gasped. "You can't be serious. Those Germans will be out looking for us. And the Horn is the first place they'll look!"

"Do you have any better ideas, man? After these fine threads we bought, we got two dollars and thirty cents left. Unless you got some bread you ain't told me about."

"But we can't go to the Horn as long as they're looking for us," I protested. "Unless . . ."

"Unless what?"

"Unless we turn the mothers in," I said.

"Jeez, Richie," said Matty shaking his head. "Once you get an idea in your head, it sure ain't in your feet. I think we shouldn't mess with those dudes. We almost got killed today." He pushed away his coffee cup and began tracing designs on the table top with his spoon handle. "And we're right back to where we were when you wanted to tail them last night. Now we don't even have any I.D. at all, let alone stuff from 1976. They'd most likely take us away."

"We could call them and tip them off at the police station," I said.

"No way. We can't tell the cops anything but what they look like. You don't think they'll be hanging around that pad on East 88th, just waiting to be picked up, do you? Don't forget, they think we're government agents. That's why I think it'll be cool to go to the Horn. Those guys don't want to be picked up any more than we do. They're probably on their way out of the country now that they think they've been spotted by us junior G-men."

"All right," I said, "but we can at least tip off the authorities about what's going on."

"Darn, Richie," said Matty in exasperation, "we don't know what they got planned. Any time they got into a heavy rap about whatever-it-is, it was in German. And I only got three years of high school German."

"But they must have said something that would give us a clue."

"Sure they did. They said that stuff about fire bombs that tipped me off to begin with. The rest is all nonsense to me."

"Think, man, think," I said. "There had to be something. Maybe if you run it past me, we can figure it out."

"OK, OK," said Matty getting to his feet, "but I'm not going to do it on an empty stomach. Let's see what they got to eat here."

We got trays and went up to the counter. It was all steam-table stuff, same as in school. But I've tasted worse. The price for meat loaf, two veggies and bread, butter and gravy came to thirty-five cents apiece.

Once we had dinner, we ran over the whole thing all over again. All we could piece together was that these dudes were going to fire bomb something big, very soon. But what and where, we couldn't figure.

"Wait a minute," said Matty. "I do remember a place they mentioned. They kept talking about eighty-eight. I thought at first they meant where we were, at 88th Street. But they didn't say *Strasse* after the eighty-eight. They said something else. I never heard the word before. Oh, and one other thing. They kept talking about Lafayette something."

"Lafayette Street!" I almost shouted. "It's downtown!"

"What's on Lafayette Street to bomb?" asked Matty. "In fact, what's on Lafayette Street, period?"

"Well, police headquarters is on Lafayette Street," I began.

"Sure, sure," grinned Matty. "They're going to burn police headquarters. You think they'll ask the chief of police for a match, too?"

I had to admit it was ridiculous. We gave up on it, then. Or really, Matty did. It was still bothering me, especially that Lafayette reference. But as Matty said, life goes on. We had to eat and get a place to sleep. And Matty had a job, maybe.

It turned out to be not a maybe at all. When the Horn opened, Johnny Rogers made the deal firm. Matty was a steady drummer with the band. Seventy bucks a week. I have to hand it to Matty. No sooner had he and Johnny Rogers shaken hands on the deal, when he hit Rogers up for an advance on his salary.

He ran Rogers the tale that we were from out of town and tapped for cash, which was true enough. But he didn't say just how far out of town we were really from. Rogers broke his heart and advanced Matty fifteen bucks. Big deal. He even made a point of telling Matty how paying him more than ten bucks showed that he trusted Matty to show up next night.

The money wasn't cold in his hand when he slipped me the ten.

"Listen, man," he said, "this is just a grind until the

guests start coming in. Get us a coupla rooms at the Y. Come back and pick me up after work, OK?"

"Gotcha," I said.

I got a funny look at the Y when I came in dressed the way I was. But I explained to the desk clerk that Matty and I were out-of-towners and had been mugged. I told him Matty would be in after four o'clock in the morning, and I wanted to get cleaned up. The desk clerk looked me over and gave me a funny look.

"I'm not surprised," he said. "Why don't you use our steam bath? It's free, you know. I'm off duty in an hour. I might even see you there."

I gave the dude behind the desk a hard look. Yeah, just like I thought. Some things in New York never change. I made sure that I was in and out of the Y's steam room and pool and back in my room before an hour was up.

But I was really whipped. The steam and swim had relaxed me so much, I didn't want to put my dirty clothes back on. I didn't want to do anything but get some sleep. I called Matty at the Horn from the pay station on my floor. I told him his room number and to get the key at the desk when he got in. Then I went to bed and crashed.

What a bummer. I dreamed the whole creepy episode all night long. Except when Strong Boy was ready to wring my neck in those hands of his, I'd wake up. By the time I got to sleep for good, it was after two o'clock in the morning. Or at least that's what the desk clerk told me on the house phone. And the dreams came back again.

I woke with a start and drenched in sweat. The sun was coming in my window. The dreams of the night came crowding back into my consciousness. Then it hit me. I knew what the spies had been talking about! I jumped out of bed and ran down the hall to Matty's room, a towel around my waist. I didn't know what time it was. I didn't care. I pounded on Matty's door. In a minute, he opened the door, yawning.

"What's happening?" he mumbled.

"Get dressed," I said, pushing past him into the room. "I know what the Germans are up to!" I sat down on Matty's bed as he closed the door and turned to me. "When the Nazis were rapping in German, they kept mentioning Lafayette, right?"

"Right."

"Well, I just remembered. Lafayette isn't a street at all."

"Then who is it?" asked Matty, sleepily.

"Not who, what," I said excitedly. "The U.S.S. Lafayette is the name that the Allies gave to the French passenger liner Normandie when the French gave it to us, so the Hitler bunch couldn't get it. We converted it into a troop transport and called it the Lafayette. They're going to fire bomb the Normandie!"

11

Lovely Day for a Drive

"Hold on," said Matty, "we don't know where the Normandie is!"

"Sure, we do," I ran on. "It's right here in New York. I remember it real clearly from history class. Mr. Robbins said that it was the first major act of German sabotage in World War II. The government denied it was sabotage because of morale on the home front. But the Normandie . . ." I sat down again. I realized what I was saying.

"The Normandie what?" said Matty, still waiting for me to finish.

"The Normandie burned and capsized at Pier 88 in Manhattan on February 9th, 1942," I recited, just like on the history test I'd taken two weeks ago, or thirty-four years from now, depending on how you looked at it. "And don't bother to get dressed, Matty."

"Are you nuts?" he gasped. "Maybe we can still head them off. Did anyone get killed in the fire?"

"Yeah," I said dully. "But don't you see? It doesn't

matter. If we studied it in history, it happened. We can't change that. You might as well get some sleep, Matt."

Matty ran his hands over his face, then sat in the chair next to the bed. He had his dirty shirt still in his hand, ready to throw on. I glanced at it.

"Did you work in that shirt last night?" I asked.

Matty looked at his shirt in his hand, like he just noticed it. "Yeah. It didn't show too much. Johnny gave me a band jacket to wear. It covered most of the dirt. Didn't fit any better than my new topcoat."

He dropped the shirt on the floor and began walking around the room in his underwear.

"Look," he said turning and facing me, "you say that the boat burned, anyway."

"Right."

"And there's nothing we can do to stop it, right?"

"You got it, babe."

"Well, what about the Nazis? Did they get caught, at least?"

"Nobody knows. Mr. Robbins says that the government hushed the whole thing up. They even denied it was sabotage. So, naturally, there's no record of them being caught, even if they were. If it comes to that, Mr. Robbins says we don't even know for sure what happened at Pearl Harbor. There's been some talk about looking into that, after all these years."

Matty started getting into his shirt, and looked around for his shoes.

"What are you doing?" I asked. "I told you we can't help it."

"Dummy!" said Matty. "If the books don't say anything about the saboteurs being caught, maybe they were actually caught, after all. And maybe, just maybe, we were the guys that did it! Come on, we gotta find Pier 88!"

It was half-past two by the lobby clock when we got

downstairs, dressed and ready to run. We were halfway out the door when I realized we didn't know where we were going. I dashed back to the desk. The same guy was on. As I came up to the desk, he gave me a look and said, "I missed you in the steam room."

"Never mind," I said. "Where's Pier 88?"

"Where's Pier 88? On the Hudson, naturally. At 48th Street, I think."

"Thanks," I said. I checked the lobby clock again. "Is that the right time?" I asked, over my shoulder and going away.

"No!" he shouted after me. "It's really half-past three, war time. We changed it at two this morning to an hour ahead. President's order . . ."

I didn't get the rest. We were out the door and looking for a cab. We hailed one right on Central Park West and gave the address to the driver. He took off like a snail.

"Can't you move this thing any faster?" I shouted at the driver. "We have to get to Pier 88 right away."

The driver didn't change his speed at all.

"You and the rest of New York City, bub," he said over his shoulder. "Don't worry. It's still burning."

"What is?" I asked, afraid I already knew the answer.

"The Normandie. Where you been? It's on the radio and everything. Listen, kid. I'm gonna haveta drop youse on Eleventh Avenue. You can't get any closer on accounta the fire engines and all . . ."

"Get us there just the same, turkey," snapped Matty.

"Who d'you think yer talkin' to, nigger?" lipped the driver, pulling over.

I looked up at the signpost on the corner. We were at 51st Street and Ninth Avenue. It wasn't any time to get into a hassle. I threw open the door when the cab pulled over, and Matty and I jumped out.

"Whaddeyez doin'?" shouted the cabby. "Youse guys owe me sixty cents. You want I should call a cop?"

I reached into my ratty coat pocket and took out our last one dollar bill and threw it at him.

"Keep the change, mother!" I hollered and took off with Matty down the street.

We saw the smoke and heard the sirens two blocks away. The cabbie was right about one thing. The police had the blocks approaching 49th and 50th Streets shut off and were directing traffic around the area. The streets were full of rubberneckers, trying to see some flames or blood. I guess New Yorkers haven't changed too much in thirty-four years.

We got past a couple of police barricades and made it down to the elevated highway that ran along Twelfth Avenue, the West Side Drive. It looked like every fire engine and fire boat in the city was on the scene. All of them were pouring tons of water on the Normandie, but what it was doing, I couldn't see. I scanned the crowds lining the far side of Twelfth Avenue and . . .

"Look, Matty!" I cried. "There they are!"

Sure enough. In with the crowds and dressed as workmen, complete to their I.D. badges on their woolen shirts, were Strong Boy and Ski Instructor. If the Colonel was around, I didn't see him. Matty saw where I was pointing. But so did Strong Boy. They started to pull back into the crowd. It was right out of an old movie. I pointed at them from across the street and hollered to the crowd, "Stop those men! They set the fire!"

Ski Instructor broke and ran. Strong Boy hesitated for a split second, then followed. They seemed to be heading for 50th Street and the police barriers. Matty and I pounded after them. But they had a good half-block's lead on us. You'd have thought some citizen would have tried to help stop them, but no. The good citizens of

New York did it in typical New York style. They watched while we chased the Nazis.

Strong Boy and his blond buddy jumped the barriers and ran like heck for a black Hudson sedan parked nearby. They were inside with the motor going before we reached the barrier, where there was a police car parked. I was ready to stop running. I figured we'd lost them, but Matty kept going, and so did I. He reached the barrier ahead of me, vaulted it and opened the door to the vacant police car.

"What are you doing?" I yelped.

"Get inside!" he rapped, fiddling around under the dashboard. "This is an old Ford. If the steering wheel isn't locked, I can jump start it with this." He held up a quarter. "Two screws right under . . . here!"

The engine jumped into noisy life. Matty did a one-hundred-eighty-degree-turn that would have made Charles Bronson jealous, and we were off after the two Nazis in the Hudson sedan.

"You're crazy, you know that, don't you?" I shouted at Matty.

"Yeah," said Matty grinning and stepping harder on the gas pedal.

We kept them in sight on a car chase up Twelfth Avenue, across 59th Street and toward the East Side. Somewhere along the way, Matty found the switch for the siren on the hot cop car we were in. After that, it got easier going through traffic. The Nazis were still pushing hard and had gotten onto the 59th Street Bridge approach. We roared after them. At the bridge entrance, we picked up some company. Evidently, the cops knew the car had been stolen and radioed ahead of us. We swept by them and, sirens blaring, they came after us.

There were more of them waiting on the other side. They'd set up a barrier. But they didn't know about the

Hudson with the Germans inside. They whipped past at an easy sixty miles an hour. We were so close at this point, the cops couldn't cut us off. In a few seconds, we had two more cop cars after us.

I felt a stinging sensation on the back of my neck. I turned and saw a neat, starred hole in the rear window of our hot cop car.

"Matty! They're shooting at us!" I yelped.

"Then get down," he snapped, stepping on it harder. That was when Ski Instructor leaned out the passenger side of the Hudson in front of us and put a shot through the windshield, inches from Matty.

We nearly crashed right then and there. Soon as the bullet from Ski Instructor's gun hit the windshield, the whole thing cracked and crazed, obscuring the view forward. For once in my life, I did the right thing at the right time. I didn't even think about it.

There was a pump fire extinguisher on my side in a clip. I took it and used it like a club, knocked out the glass from the windshield as we tore along at sixty plus, over city streets. It worked. Matty narrowly avoided an El structure post as soon as he could see where he was at. We pressed on after the Hudson, where had now gained a block.

The wind was rushing in with the glass gone. It made some kind of a racket. Matty looked over at me for a second and said, "Thanks, Richie," and away we went after them, the cops after us.

The chase lasted I don't know how long. When things are happening that fast, you don't keep track. But, finally, I began to recognize some areas. We were in Brooklyn now, and headed for the Narrows! I shouted to Matty over the wind and the noise of our siren.

"They're heading for the Narrows. Do you know where that is?"

"Sure," hollered Matty, missing a trolley car by a coat of paint. "I been fishing with my dad off Sheepshead Bay all my life. It's not too far away."

"There's probably a sub waiting for them," I shouted. "But not in daylight, like this. Keep them in sight. We may get their hideout, too."

"If the cops don't get us first," he shouted back. "Hey, look!"

The Hudson had blown a tire. It swerved from one side of the street to the other, Strong Boy trying to keep it under control. He got it straightened out just in time to run head on into God knows how many tons of Brooklyn trolley car.

A cloud of orange flame and black smoke shot up, and the street was suddenly filled with flying pieces of the Hudson, Strong Boy and Ski Instructor. The Nazis had been evidently carrying some more explosives or incendiaries inside.

We were so close behind them that I felt the rush of hot air on my face when the Hudson blew. We were almost too close to stop. I don't know how Matty did it, but he swerved around the flaming mess and over to the other side of the street. We almost hit the rear end of another trolley car, going in the other direction. I looked through what was left of the rear window. The police car immediately behind us had stopped. But two more behind him kept coming after us.

"Aren't we going to stop?" I shouted at Matty. "The saboteurs are done for now."

Matty put his foot to the floor. "Are you nuts?" he hollered back. "Those cops probably think that we set the fire. And those two guys in the Hudson aren't in any shape to confess and tell 'em different."

"But where can we go?" I hollered.

"We're going where we should have gone to begin

with," shouted Matty. "Back to Branford and Abner Pew. If nothing else, we can get out of 1942!"

I looked at the sky. It was past five o'clock now, and the sun was going down. If we could get to Branford after nightfall, there was a fighting chance that we could get into the old cemetery unseen.

Matty quickly wove the police car through a bunch of Brooklyn back streets until we came to a quiet block. He pulled over to the curb and stopped.

"C'mon, man," I said, "this is no time to stop! We have to get to Branford."

"Sure," said Matty, "in a hot police car with no windshield. We might just as well have the Branford marching band walking in front of us. We have to ditch this car and get another one."

"But how?" I wailed.

"Be quiet, and let me think," came back Matty. "Seems we've been doing everything but using our heads lately. For instance, we've been thinking we're stuck in 1942. We never have been. We can't go back to our own Time, it's true. But who's to say we can't go back even further into the Past? It's sure not getting us back home, but it's better than where we are. But right now, what we really need is another car. Maybe if we . . . hey, Rich, look!"

I followed the direction Matty was pointing in. Just rounding the corner of the quiet block we'd parked on, came an honest-to-God model 816 Cord phaeton. It pulled over and parked not sixty feet from us. Matty started up the motor of the police car and turned on the siren.

"Are you nuts, man?" I shouted. "Turn that thing off!"

Matty only smiled and made a shhh-ing motion. "Just be quiet and let me talk," he said as we pulled up alongside the Cord.

The guy was just locking his door as Matty came bouncing out of the police car. I have to hand it to Matty. He did it all so fast that the owner of the Cord never had time to think things out. In one motion, Matty took the guy's car keys and had the door opened. He slid behind the wheel as I went to the door on the other side, already open.

"Police officers," said Matty to the startled citizen. "We're after saboteurs, and we need your car!"

Matty had the car in gear and we were halfway down the block and turning the corner before I even had the nerve to look back. The guy was still standing at the curbside, watching us drive off. He had such a dumb look on his face, I couldn't help but laugh. Matty, too.

"Don't get too happy, Rich," said Matty after we both finished laughing. "It's only a matter of minutes before he realizes he's been had. Then he's going to call the cops."

"Well step on it, then!" I said. "The quicker we get there, the better."

"Uh-uh," said Matty, driving at what seemed like a crawl. "We go nice and slow. We're not driving a hot car until that dude calls the police. In the meantime, we don't need to get picked up for speeding, do we?"

We made it almost to Branford on 25-A before the cops spotted us again. But running away from a police cruiser in what we were driving turned out to be no problem at all. The 816 Cord was not only the prettiest car of its day, but it was supercharged. When the siren sounded behind us, Matty put the gas pedal to the floor. It felt like when Matty had kicked apart the chair I'd been tied to. The Cord took off like a goosed antelope, and soon the police car disappeared behind us. As a further break, it was getting toward nightfall.

We made it, but not by much. By the time we got to Branford Avenue, there were three cops ahead of us and two cars behind us. It may have been thirty-four years in the past, but the cops had their chase patterns worked out.

I think what saved us was that even though streets had changed some in Branford, it was still the same town we'd both grown up in. The terrain was still the same; it wouldn't change. We swung around in a loop and into the woods adjoining the cemetery. We were still minutes ahead of the nearest cops. And blessedly, it had turned dark.

We ditched the Cord and made it on foot through the woods. We climbed the fence surrounding the cemetery and in a short time, we were standing in front of Abner Pew's gravestone. Not that it helped. The only things moving in the darkened cemetery were me, Matty, and the cops. We could see the beams of their flashlights at the main gate. It would be just a matter of time before we were found.

"Matty, he's not here," I whispered. "What are we gonna do?"

"Don't ask me," he answered. "I just ran out of ideas. But you better think of something to tell those cops when they find us. That is, if they don't shoot first and ask questions later."

I looked over my shoulder toward the main gate. The flashlight beams were moving in a definite pattern. The police were checking out the cemetery in an orderly search plan, row by row. I figured we had maybe five minutes before we were found. I felt like Matty. All used up and no more fight left. It was a good idea Matty had. But evidently it was too early in the night for Abner Pew to show up. I sat down on the edge of Abner Pew's stone. I was whipped and I knew it.

I know it sounds weird, but at that moment, I thought of Sheila. Don't ask me why. But it was like a light bulb went on over my head, just like in a comic strip. Both ideas came at the same time.

"Matty?"

"Yeah, Rich."

"I just remembered. When I called Sheila, I called the wrong number. She told me HE 3–5694. I dialed HE 3–5649. I know I did. She didn't lie to me after all!"

"Oh, wow!" Matty exploded. "Here we are about to be shot for saboteurs, and you're thinking of chicks! Richie, you're one in a million. You really are . . ."

"Keep your voice down," I hissed. "They'll hear us. I got an idea."

But it was too late. When Matty had blown up, the flashlight beams stopped moving. I could hear the cops' voices now.

"Where's that coming from?"

"Over there, from the old part of the cemetery."

A whistle began to blow, and the searching lights probed through the night in our direction. I had to talk fast.

"Matty. Let's do the drill for going back into the Past. You know, the way we got back here."

I heard Matty slap his forehead in exasperation.

"Of course!" he said. "I should have thought of it myself. We don't need Pew to get through the Gate."

The flashlight beam caught us full as we stood. We were facing Pew's stone, and the lights caught us from behind.

"All right, you Nazi bastards," said a voice from behind the lights, "reach for the sky. If you make a wrong move, I'll shoot!"

"Matty," I whispered, "we're facing Pew's stone. If we move two paces forward and turn and walk, we'll be through the Gate."

"Yeah, and if we move one pace, this cop is gonna blow us away," he answered.

"He's bound to have us turn around. If we can move the two paces first, we can get out of this yet."

"I'm game."

We took the chance. We moved forward two paces, still keeping our hands in the air. When the shot came, I involuntarily pulled my neck into my shoulders, as if that would have helped. But I wasn't hurt. The cop had fired into the air.

"I said 'hold it'," came the voice behind the searchlight. "Next time, I'll let you have it. Now turn around and walk toward the light so I can see you better."

Matty and I looked at each other and grinned.

"I guess we better do what the man says," smiled Matty.

"I guess so," I grinned.

"No monkey business now," said the cop as we walked toward him, "or I'll . . ."

We never found out what the "or" was. As we took the third step, the light vanished. I suppose so far as the cop was concerned, so did we. Standing in front of us in bright moonlight stood the great bulk of Abner Pew.

"Well, young masters," he rumbled, "ye seem to have had a bit of trouble in 1942."

Matty and I didn't answer. We were too busy laughing and pounding each other on the back in congratulation. We both sank to the ground. It was the first time we'd stopped running in what seemed like days. When we finally stopped horsing around, we faced Abner Pew, who regarded us balefully.

"It were not a seemly thing ye did, going through the Gate whilst I was, er . . . celebrating," said Abner Pew. "Ye were lucky the local police did not slay ye on the spot. Can ye now see the consequences of entering the Gate if ye be not a True Traveler?"

I was about to say how right he was, but Matty cut in.

"Who are these True Travelers you keep talking about, Abner? What do they do? And *why* do they travel in Time?"

Pew hesitated and blew his nose on a handkerchief he took from his sleeve. It sounded like a low D on a trombone.

"Ye need not know," he said with finality. "But ye cannot stay here, either, though I be glad for the company and conversation."

"Well, what can we do?" I asked. "We can't go back to 1942. They're combing the countryside for us as Nazi saboteurs."

"Ye can only pass through the Gate to yet another time in the Past," Pew replied. "Ye may not remain here too much longer. Unless, like myself, ye wish to become Gatekeeper. S'truth, it would not grieve me to be quit of m'duties. After two hundred years, I grow weary."

I swallowed hard. The prospect of spending the next century or so in Branford Memorial Park wasn't my idea of a good time.

"But what time in the Past can we go to?" I asked. "I thought I knew the '40's, but it turned out I didn't at all. Abner, I don't know about any other period in history as well as I know the '40's."

"Then ye may remain and guard the Gate," said Pew, smiling broadly.

He began unbuckling the wide belt that circled his greatcoat. I heard the keys jingle. The full set was there again! But the Nazis had taken my iron key when they'd got my wallet and money.

"I see ye be staring at my keys," said Abner Pew. "Yes, once the key to the Future Gate left your possession, it returned straightaway to my ring here." He patted the keys at his waist. "It will do the same for you lads once I'm gone . . ."

"Hey, wait a sec!" put in Matty. "Don't take it off. I can't speak for Richie, but no way I'm gonna stay here. I'll take my chances on the Past."

Pew turned to me.

"Well, young Master Richard, will ye stay, or no? Speak, for ye have little time before the while ye may remain within the Gate."

It wasn't a choice.

"I'll go with Matty," I said, feeling less in command of things than I sounded. "But can you give us the Future Gate Key again, Abner? I think I can find the Gate to the Future."

Pew favored us with a smile.

"I thought ye might, for I gave ye the instructions."

"I didn't think you'd remember," I said. "When we last saw you, you were kinda . . ."

"I were drunk as a lord," said Pew, amiably. "But that is not to say I were stupid. Abner Pew, drunk or sober, I be. And though I have been a fool in the Past, it were only that emotions clouded my judgment."

He unsnapped the big iron key from his ring.

"Here, young Master Gilroy. And I wish ye luck in the Past. But ye must go now. It's time. Turn and walk, as I've shown ye."

Not wanting to take a chance on staying, Matty and I turned and walked. The moonlight in the graveyard vanished. It was a moonless night, wherever we were. And thank heavens it was warm out. Wherever, or when-ever we were now, it was summertime.

Just then, the moon came out. It had been behind some clouds. I could see Matty clearly. The area around us looked the same, but that was no surprise. It hadn't looked that different in 1776.

"What year do you think this is, Matt?" I asked.

"Don't ask me," he replied. "I'm just thankful it ain't 1942, is all."

"Amen!" I breathed. "But it would be handy to know what year Pew sent us to. We didn't tell him any particu-lar time."

Then as from a long, long distance, we heard the dia-pason bass of Abner Pew, "It be June, the year of our Lord, nineteen hundred and twelve . . ."

My head spun. My mind began racing. What did I

know about 1912? It was pre-World War I. The only real jazz then was way down in New Orleans. Louis Armstrong was only a little boy. The big craze in our part of the country was ragtime. Matty gave me a look as if to say, "You ready to go?"

I nodded, and with Matty alongside me, we walked toward the cemetery gate.

ABOUT THE AUTHOR

T. ERNESTO BETHANCOURT is also known as singer-guitarist Tom Paisley, who began his career in coffeehouses in Greenwich Village in the sixties, performing with then unknowns Bob Dylan, Bill Cosby and Peter, Paul, and Mary. He has served as a contributing editor to *High Fidelity Magazine*, and is the author of the highly acclaimed young adult novels, *New York City Too Far from Tampa Blues*, *The Dog Days of Arthur Cane*, *The Mortal Instruments*, *Tune In Yesterday*, and *Dr. Doom: Superstar*. He lives in Huntington Beach, California, with his wife and two daughters.

DAHL, ZINDEL, BLUME AND BRANCATO

Select the best names, the best stories in the world of teenage and young readers books!

☐ 12143 CHARLIE AND THE CHOCOLATE FACTORY $1.95
       Roald Dahl

☐ 12144 CHARLIE AND THE GREAT GLASS $1.95
       ELEVATOR Roald Dahl

☐ 15035 DANNY THE CHAMPION OF THE WORLD $1.95
       Roald Dahl

☐ 15032 JAMES AND THE GIANT PEACH Roald Dahl $2.25

☐ 12154 THE WONDERFUL STORY OF HENRY $1.95
       SUGAR AND SIX MORE Roald Dahl

☐ 14657 THE PIGMAN Paul Zindel $2.25

☐ 12774 I NEVER LOVED YOUR MIND Paul Zindel $1.95

☐ 14836 PARDON ME, YOU'RE STEPPING ON MY $2.25
       EYEBALL! Paul Zindel

☐ 12741 MY DARLING, MY HAMBURGER $1.95
       Paul Zindel

☐ 11829 CONFESSIONS OF A TEENAGE BABOON $1.95
       Paul Zindel

☐ 13628 IT'S NOT THE END OF THE WORLD $1.95
       Judy Blume

☐ 13693 WINNING Robin Brancato $1.95

☐ 12171 SOMETHING LEFT TO LOSE $1.75
       Robin Brancato

☐ 12953 BLINDED BY THE LIGHT Robin Brancato $1.95

Buy them at your local bookstore or use this handy coupon for ordering:

TEENAGERS FACE LIFE AND LOVE

Choose books filled with fun and adventure, discovery and disenchantment, failure and conquest, triumph and tragedy, life and love.

☐	13359	**THE LATE GREAT ME** Sandra Scoppettone	$1.95
☐	13691	**HOME BEFORE DARK** Sue Ellen Bridgers	$1.75
☐	13671	**ALL TOGETHER NOW** Sue Ellen Bridgers	$1.95
☐	14836	**PARDON ME, YOU'RE STEPPING ON MY EYEBALL!** Paul Zindel	$2.25
☐	11091	**A HOUSE FOR JONNIE O.** Blossom Elfman	$1.95
☐	14306	**ONE FAT SUMMER** Robert Lipsyte	$1.95
☐	13184	**I KNOW WHY THE CAGED BIRD SINGS** Maya Angelou	$2.25
☐	12650	**QUEEN OF HEARTS** Bill & Vera Cleaver	$1.75
☐	12741	**MY DARLING, MY HAMBURGER** Paul Zindel	$1.95
☐	13555	**HEY DOLLFACE** Deborah Hautzig	$1.75
☐	13897	**WHERE THE RED FERN GROWS** Wilson Rawls	$2.25
☐ ☐	11829	**CONFESSIONS OF A TEENAGE BABOON** Paul Zindel	$1.95
☐	14730	**OUT OF LOVE** Hilma Wolitzer	$1.75
☐	14225	**SOMETHING FOR JOEY** Richard E. Peck	$2.25
☐	14687	**SUMMER OF MY GERMAN SOLDIER** Bette Greene	$2.25
☐	13693	**WINNING** Robin Brancato	$1.95
☐	13628	**IT'S NOT THE END OF THE WORLD** Judy Blume	$1.95

Buy them at your local bookstore or use this handy coupon for ordering:

Bantam Book Catalog

Here's your up-to-the-minute listing of over 1,400 titles by your favorite authors.

This illustrated, large format catalog gives a description of each title. For your convenience, it is divided into categories in fiction and non-fiction—gothics, science fiction, westerns, mysteries, cookbooks, mysticism and occult, biographies, history, family living, health, psychology, art.

So don't delay—take advantage of this special opportunity to increase your reading pleasure.

Just send us your name and address and 50¢ (to help defray postage and handling costs).

BANTAM BOOKS, INC.
Dept. FC, 414 East Golf Road, Des Plaines, Ill. 60016

Mr./Mrs./Miss_____
(please print)

Address_____

City_____State_____Zip_____

Do you know someone who enjoys books? Just give us their names and addresses and we'll send them a catalog too!

_____

Mr./Mrs./Miss_____

Address_____

City_____State_____Zip_____

_____

Mr./Mrs./Miss_____

Address_____

City_____State_____Zip_____

FC—9/78